M̶o̶t̶h̶e̶r̶ ̶L̶o̶v̶e̶s̶

Blue Flowers

("something in the grass?")

A Mary Randolph Adventure

Margaret P Nelson

Margaret P. Nelson

Oct 2014

1

Mother Loves Blue Flowers

First Edition 2014

This is a fictional account of events and characters that are entirely creations of the author's imagination. Any similarities to any persons living or dead, names, actual places or events are entirely coincidental.

ISBN Number: **978-1-49523-831-4**

Library of Congress Control Number: 2014902028

Illustrations by James Simcox

Website... www.thegirlfromtheditchdumproad.com

Agat Bay Publishing
Greenville, Missouri

A few years ago, a little country girl stepped out of the past and demanded my attention, Mary Randolph.

Sharing Mary's adventures has opened a world I didn't expect, a world where Mary and I take a few friends along with us on our trips. I would like to thank my friends and readers who have patiently listened to my efforts to put these stories on paper. Gratitude to so many wonderful people would be a long and tedious affair, but I have been given special support by many kind people, and my thanks goes to them all. Bless you readers, bridge players, old friends and dear folk, library folks, and fellow writers. [Mary would say so, too!]

Probably no one has taught me more than my dogs, bark like crazy to get to where you want to be; but remember to chase a few rabbits along the way.

DEDICATION

This book is especially lovingly dedicated to Jim. He has been my editor, my extensive spell check, my mentor, my tormentor and my fellow adventurer. I could have never finished without his patience, teasing and obsessive attention to detail.

This book is also dedicated to my two sons, Fred Nelson and David Nelson.

Margaret P Nelson

Mother Loves Blue Flowers

A Mary Randolph Mystery/Adventure

Margaret P Nelson

Table of Contents
Mother Loves Blue Flowers

PROLOGUE

"something in the grass?"

Horses, though used for many years strictly as working partners to men, are an enrichment to the rural pastures. The beauty of a softly flowering meadow is only enhanced by horses chasing each other with manes flowing, frolicking on long gangly legs that turn into sheer grace when they run. Their gambols over a country meadow are long looping circles, through deep grasses, ferns and wildflowers. The lacy Queen Anne's Lace, and the wild daisies dance under their feet, and the periwinkle blue chicory blooms flirt with the flashing hooves. Sometimes the chicory flowers part before them to let the white shining bleached bones that are beneath the plants show through, and..., sometimes the horses even notice the blue flowers that bloom from the eyeholes of the aged horse skulls that dot their pastures.

In the past, dishonest horse dealers were known to give aging, decrepit horses doses of arsenic. The arsenic acts like a fountain of youth for past-their-prime animals. The horse is a colt again, with sparkling eyes, frolicking ways and a shiny coat! He is all that you would want in a vigorous, healthy horse.

Unfortunately, in a short time, these wild, spirited, healthy horses suddenly transform back into the old, tired horses that they are, and in a few days, the buyer will have the job of burying a horse that had seemed to be in such wonderful health a few days before, wondering what was in the grass of his pasture that kills his livestock.

Chapter 1

SIDEBAR FOR HARLAND AND THE SHERIFF

Spring, 1958

"Dammit!!... Now don't call me *Harland!* When I have these robes on, - even just here in my chamber - if I am wearing the robes of this court of the state of Missouri, I am *Judge Phillips*"!

The sheriff sighed. "Sorry, Harland. I know you have had a long hard day with all this stuff that is going on, and, I guess me bringing one more little problem in to you is just the final raindrop in your barrel." The sheriff paused and smiled. "Tell you what. It's after hours, why don't you take off that robe and put on your comfortable shoes, and I will see if I can figure out where you hide your booze. Just willing to bet this long arm of the law can sniff that stuff out for us."

A few minutes, later, "The Judge" had gone away for the day; the robe was hung in the closet, and Harland Phillips had settled in his comfortable chair behind the desk with his worn old boots propped on the judicial desk. Sighing, he sipped some of Tennessee's finest, and grinned at his friend, the Sheriff.

"Now, let me get this straight. You have a farmer wanting to file a complaint because his neighbor is a witch and has been putting hexes on him that are killing his horses. And, you are worried about him getting those peckerheads in the white sheets out there after her some night, if you don't put a lid on this."

Appreciative sip. "Got to thank you for bringing this in, sort of makes my day seem less crazy!" Harland gave a less than dignified snort around his whiskey. "And I would be willing to bet you are trying to figure out which one of those damned government forms you have to fill out for a case like this?!"

"I know, Harland. You wouldn't believe some of the stories I get that never get to your court. Folks seem to think I am a sort of dumping ground for everything from bad sex to hit-and-runs."

"Whoa! Bad sex? Now that is one that has never made it to my court. What's that all about?"

"Well, there's this lady in town. I won't mention her name; you might see her in here someday. She was in my office awhile back complaining that her husband was sort of sick all the time, and slept a lot and never took an interest in her anymore. Told her to go home and start dressing like her cute teenaged daughters and be friendly to him and maybe that would help. Couldn't tell her to drop about twenty pounds and quit nagging the poor guy, but..."

Very non-judicial snicker. "Well, how did that work out?"

"Actually, she did drop about twenty pounds! And has been dressing like her cute daughters. But she doesn't seem to hang around home with the old grouch much these days. Saw her out with another guy, parked out on the ditch dump road a couple of Saturday nights ago. Looked like they were taking care of that little problem of hers just fine. I figured it wasn't really any of my business, until one of them got mad and wanted to file a complaint, and that didn't look likely, at the time. Besides of which, I would hate to think what kind of forms I would have to file for that sort of thing!"

Harland stretched his booted feet on the desk and grinned at his friend. "Okay, besides your mysterious lady with an itch, what else is going on out there that you don't want to bother me with?"

CHAPTER 2

HIGH SCHOOL INCARCERATION

Mary..., Mary Randolph! What the heck am I doing back here?

Study hall was as boring as ever, I thought, resting my head on an elbow, propped on the graffiti carved and inked on, old wooden desk in front of me. Of course, the carved message on the old desk provided some entertainment for me. According to the stuff in the carved heart, "J.A loved P.C.", and, it was even inked in there to last forever. The angry ink marks slashed over the carved heart at a later date had me thinking. Did P.C. not return that affection, or had J.A. proved fickle and moved on to someone else? I would have to check on that, and see if a forest of J.A.'s romantic art works were scattered around the study hall.

And how old were those carvings? This was an old school with old desks. Were J.A. and P.C. smugly celebrating ten years of wedded bliss? Or even twenty-five years? And, were they still happy, or had J.A. been carving on someone else's desk? Worse yet, had he been caught in the act of carving on someone else's desk!?

My brain was busy with these musing thoughts, while my eyes were gazing, blank eyed at the teacher's aide's, in the front of the room. I had been reading about the idea of "black holes" in space, sort of dead zones, and this study hall seemed to have captured that well. All through my high school years it had been an overly gloomy sort of cavern with chalk dust and sweaty teenager smells heavy in the air and even though I had been gone for awhile, it hadn't grown any more interesting, or less smelly.

Gone for awhile? More like I had escaped into the real world but now was back in incarceration for a few more endless months of my young life.

I had finished writing the journal I had promised to turn in to the principal. Then, humming, under my breath so as not to incur the frown of the study hall teacher, to get the tune right, had written all the lyrics I could remember to that new tune I had heard on the school bus radio last evening, "Rock Around the Clock". Liked the foot tapping it inspired, but was sure it was one that my father would not appreciate hearing blasting out of our little plastic Bendix radio in the kitchen at home.

Then, still stuck in an endless bubble of time that the large clock at the front of the study hall seemed to have trapped us all, students and teacher in, I had done a quick forbidden crossword puzzle in one of the library newspapers. I felt a little indignant burn over the two by four card over the newspapers instructing readers not to mark or cut newspapers. Why have daily newspapers if not to read and use? And this paper was over two weeks old, anyway! Still, when I returned it, I carefully folded the paper so that the marked up puzzle was not too noticeable on the hanging wood rack.

Now, bored with watching the impossibly slow-moving clock hands, I continued looking around the room at my fellow inmates in the torturous hour long lock-up.

The center of the little group in the front of the study hall, of course, was Judy.

It was always Judy...

Since my favorite friend, Ruby, had died, I had tried to make a conscious effort to be nice to Judy. I often, somewhat unkindly, thought of her as being a silly, spoiled person, but sometimes, there seemed to be something a little more to her personality than just that. An unhappy, soul-felt loneliness seemed to lurk in the shadows behind this hair-brained, shallow-girl face, and she often seemed really grateful for my friendship, as if there was really no one else that she could trust to allow to see deeper than what was on her surface. While she seemed to most of our classmates to be a successful 1950's rock and roll teenaged girl, whose only interest was in finding an older boyfriend with a car; there were times that I sensed a sort of dark desperation behind the bobby sox and bubble gum.

Now, in the front of the study hall, Judy was holding court with some of her more impressionable minions. She was sporting a new outfit that her mom had just made her the past weekend. It had a full circle skirt that settled over her heavily starched petticoats, and twirled out in an almost thigh high fluff when she pivoted on her white moccasins and bobby socks for their admiration. Sure enough, it had the obligatory poodle on the skirt and she wore a twin angora sweater set with it, and a silky neck scarf fastened with an artificial flower spray. Her hair was pushed up on the back of her head in a style that even I liked, puffy and classic looking. Judy had told the group that it was a new thing called a "French Roll" and the reason it was so "pouffy" was because the beauty shop had "teased" it, then sprayed it so much that it was like a permanent, beautifully shaped helmet on her head. "Here, feel it; it is real hard, just like a wood carving or something!"

Her successful teenager slut look was only off-set by persistent acne blemishes that even the chalky make-up didn't quite cover. The constantly popping bubblegum also seemed to dim the mystery and beauty of the elegant upswept hair.

When the bell rang and we all started to crowd out into the hall, for the last period of the day, I smelled her bubblegum before I realized that Judy was pushing close to get in behind me and breath into my ear. "Mary, where is your last class?"

I told her.

"Good, I'll be waiting there after class when you get out. I have something private I want to talk to you about. This is real important."

Chapter 3

"SEE, I MET THIS MARINE~~~"

Sure enough, when I came out of my History of Missouri class, Judy was standing outside the door to catch me by the arm. "Cm'on, lets go down to the ladies' room to talk. I need to pee, anyway."

In the cool late afternoon dimness of the ladies' room, Judy fussed around, washing her hands, tucking in a few loose tendrils of hair under her stiff hairdo, and making kissy lips at the mirror as she re-did her lipstick. When the first bus had left with most of the kids, and we were alone, she turned to me.

"Mary, listen. I have a chance... well, I am invited, sort of, to go to the Marine Corp Ball on the base down in Memphis in about a month. See, I met this Marine on a bus coming down from St. Louis about a month ago, and we have been writing letters. He's a real nice guy, and they will come pick us up, and get a motel room for us, and take us out, and everything. It will be real nice, sort of like a homecoming weekend dance for the Marines, except they will be wearing really neat, patriotic uniforms and so forth. The only problem is that I need to bring a friend along to date one of the other boys. See, the thing is, my guy doesn't have a car, so he has to get his friend to drive him up here to pick us up and bring us back, so; he needs a date for his friend."

Wow! Going to Memphis to stay in a motel somewhere with Judy, [whom my Dad considered a teenaged slut, anyway], and go to a dance with some strange boy!? Somehow, the image of what my father would have to say to that just boggled the mind!

"Gee, Judy, I don't think I can make it. There is a lot to do on the farm this time of the year, and my grandpa just died, and I need to spend extra time with my grandma." I almost stammered, trying to figure out a way to turn her down without sounding like a little kid whose family still bossed her around.

"Oh Mary! You've got to go! This is the chance of a lifetime! You get to meet some nice Marines, and stay in a motel with me, and they will pay for everything! They look so neat, too, all dressed up in those uniforms. Honestly, Mary, you have never seen such neat creases and shiny shoes! And they smell so good! Just all aftershave and bourbon and cigarettes and just a tang of clean sweat. Just what real men should smell like, not like these farmers around here. And we might even get to see that new guy from Memphis sing at the dance! He is so great!"

I kept my head lowered and tried to focus my attention elsewhere while Judy blathered on. Pinching in the grin, I had the thought *"Oh yeah, Sonny. I never knew what his real name was, but he seems to be doing okay with his music thing."*

"You would not believe how he moves on the stage to that wild throbbing music! He looks like one of those Greek gods, with sulky dark eyes, and those big, soft, pouty lips! He just sort of reminds me of a big, old sweaty, sexy stallion, when he starts to moving to that hot sexy beat."

I had to really bite down the grin now, as I listened to her, *Yeah, and I was there when the leader, [who is REALLY sexy, if you like hot Latin men!], of the newest communist country in our hemisphere showed him how to move like that.*

"He sure gives a girl ideas, if you know what I mean!

And, listen, we could tell our parents we were going on a church campout or something."

"Well, I guess he is pretty hot, but you know, I just can't make it this time. Maybe later, but, not this trip."

Judy clenched her lower jaw and glared at her hair in the bathroom mirror. "I can't believe you'd turn this down! Here I am offering you a chance to have a really good time and all you have to do is lie to your parents a little. Everybody does it; how do you expect to ever get a boyfriend this way?!"

"But my grandpa just died, and..."

"Oh Mary! I guarantee you he would still be dead when you got back! ...Okay, forget it! But honestly, Mary you are such an innocent!"

Innocent?--Wonder what she would think if she knew I had sailed down to Cuba, helped save the free world, and had spent several romantic, starry evenings alone on the dark deck of that dark boat with this guy they were now calling the sexiest man in the world, on the radio.

Carefully keeping my eyes down, I picked up my books off the radiator and started to leave when she called after me. "You were gone an awfully long time last semester; how did you get them to let you off so long?"

Still not making eye contact, I answered over my shoulder, "I had to go on a trip with my uncle. It was sort of family business and I did some extra work to make it up to the principal."

"What sort of trip?"

"Well, it was sort of a fishing trip down south. He is real old, and just needed someone along to help him with the hooks and stuff."

"I saw your uncle in the hall that day. He was kind of cute. Uh, how old is he?"

"Well, he's really old; probably at least fifty or so."

"Oh, that old," Sigh... "Fishing, huh? Well, I wouldn't like it; putting those nasty worms on the hooks and everything. And then, what if you caught one and had to take it off the hook and then cook it? And take out the guts?! No thank you, not for me! Give me good old boneless tuna fish, fresh out of the can!"

Chapter 4

A TOWN OF BLUE FLOWERS

At the end of the school day, I ignored the kids gathering at the bus stops, and started the walk across town to the other side, where my grandma Elkins lived.

She was alone now, in her little house on a quiet lane by the railroad tracks. Grandma's house was a weathered old wooden house, with aged peeling paint. It seemed to crouch under the large nut trees that shaded it, and crowded out the sun. That sun fed sparkling yards of grass and flowers that surrounded the majority of the fussy little cookie cutter houses in the town, but Grandma's house seemed to echo with the ghosts of working class families that had lived here and left the house every morning for hard labor. Those working folk seemed to have been content to sink on the gray wooden boards of the porch to rest in the evenings after supper and work. No real time to fuss with flowers when there was so much work to be done just to live, and raise their families.

Many of more affluent homes of the town were built by the early settlers that came from places in northern Europe at some point in the town's history, and many of their houses still held traces of that carefully preserved, middle class Germanic background. Most of the lawns were neat patches of green, religiously mowed grass, enhanced with flowering shrubs and beds of carefully tended blooming low plants. Zinnias, daisies and hollyhocks waved excitedly for attention at different times of the growing year. Rose bushes, day lilies and the blue hydrangeas formed a protective mask around the bottoms of the buildings to mask the less-than-pretty crawl spaces under the houses that nested in these floral aprons. Plant boxes blossomed in the windows, and on the carefully painted porches. Sparkling windows behind tied-back, ruffled curtains held shelf displays of treasured colored glass vases and dime store ceramics marked "Made in Japan" for all the passersby to marvel at and envy. If this town had been set down intact in the Alps mountains, for example, it would have fit in well with the postcard prettiness of the country. Except for the cheap new Japanese ceramics in the windows, our small town of neatly mowed yards and fussy little houses echoed the pictures of the rebuilding of Europe that were sometimes featured in the "Look" magazines at the library.

Somehow, though, I always had the uncomfortable feeling that some of the self-righteous attitudes of these folks lacked any basic kindness and that the flowers masked a coldness of heart as well as they masked the ugly bases upon which the houses set. I had to wonder if pretending not to see what was going on with neighbors in trouble, but rather peering out from behind the safety of lacy curtains, was a trait of denial that had crossed the Atlantic from the old countries in Europe, along with the fondness for the dark blue larkspurs and lupines crowding around the puffy beauty of the sky blue hydrangea bushes. There seemed to be an evil way of thinking that went with these townsfolk, as if their curtains covered their hearts as well as their sparkling windows. When I occasionally passed folks sitting on their porches or working in their yards, they would smile and nod apple-cheek friendly; but I was aware of an underlying ripple of holier--than-thou, and a sniffing, sideways look under lowered eyelids at strangers. Strange that they counted a country girl walking through the town as a stranger, but I sometimes felt I was as alien to them as if I had been from Cincinnati or some other exotic port. I was sort of reminded of those books I had just read about the odd little Hobbit people who lived in their shire and were totally happy to be there all their lives and never wonder about or care for other folks from outside of their world.

Even though Grandma was very quiet these days with Grandpa gone, I looked forward to these evenings I got to be with her. After a dinner of the chili that she kept on the back of her wood burning stove on nights she knew I was coming, we washed up the dishes; then went out to sit in the purple evening.

Sometimes we talked, and sometimes

she even told me things I needed to know. Sometimes, we were just quiet with a sort of unspoken communication going on between us. But now, with her silent grief staining the air between us, her sorrow made me want to distract her from that ache of pain. She sat, smiling at me, but without speaking, while I sat on the porch turning up cards from her worn, greasy deck.

To fill in the quiet, and hoping to amuse her, I kept up an almost childish patter. "Funny, when Lucy turns them over, I know what she has, but I can't make them come up by myself. Doesn't matter; I don't have to be smarter than the cards, just smarter than my sister." I smiled at my own joke, and continued turning over the cards.

Grandma watched me for a few minutes. "You aren't really controlling those cards, you know. You are just picking up on what your little sister is thinking when she turns the cards over. That is because you and she are very close. We have lots of parts of our brain that we never use, and are a little afraid to use, because people will probably think we are strange. You are just clicking into the part of your brain that understands what people around you are thinking. Maybe something in the way they are talking, or standing, or something in the back of their eyes that you aren't afraid to let yourself understand. Indians are good at that, because our ancestors lived by hunting, so we learned to understand the animals and what they were going to do next; but we also respected them because they are fellow travelers on a path through this world."

 ## Chapter 5

A JOB OPPORTUNITY FOR MARY

The next morning was Saturday, and I knew that my father would be coming into town to pick me up sometime in the morning to take me back to the farm. I spent some time, helping Grandma pull weeds out of her garden, and then settled on the front porch with her to shell peas and wait for my dad.

The vehicle that pulled up the loose gravel side lane to her house was not my dad's truck, though. Even with the heavy coat of rural Missouri soil that it was wearing, it was easy to read the state logo and see the hand-painted sheriff's star gleaming through the dust on the wooden side panel.

"Morning, Mrs. Tennie, Mary. Mary, your dad asked me if I could give you a ride home, so here I am, running a sort of police taxi service."

The old sheriff's grin was light and friendly, but I felt like there was something more that he could have said, and wasn't going to.

Evidently my grandma thought so too, as she sort of waited, then finally, reluctantly, said "Well, it is nice of you to help, and I guess if her dad wanted you to, it is okay, but where did you see him? I know they don't have a phone out there."

The sheriff's determined friendliness never wavered. "No, ma'am, but I was out there on some routine stuff and stopped on the road by the barn to talk to him. Since I have another errand to run out that way, it seemed like the thing to do, offering to give her a ride to save him having to clean up and come into town."

"Grandma, I'll come over some time next week and stay overnight, again. Sorry I have to leave now, but since Sheriff Olsen is nice enough to offer me a ride, I guess I better go."

As we pulled away, I could see my grandma frowning in the dust behind us, then, she turned and walked back into the house, with her age riding her thin, slumped shoulders.

The sheriff drove carefully back to the center of town, for awhile without speaking, then reached over and turned the Slim Whitman "Indian Love Call" on the radio, down. "I wanted to talk to you about something I'd like you to do."

He paused and seemed to try to think of a way to begin.

"Mary, do you think your dad would let you sort of ride along with me on some of my calls? Wouldn't be often, but sometimes I run up against things where I could use you. You always just seem like a dumb kid, but I've noticed you know how to ask questions that folks will answer without feeling scared of my uniform and badge. Honestly, when I ask them stuff, they must feel like they are going to be arrested or something, and I just never get anywhere with them."

Sideways glance. "I could maybe talk to the mayor, and maybe we could even get a little salary going for you, just on a part time basis, you know, that would have to come out of the cities miscellaneous funds. I wouldn't want folks to consider you a deputy or anything official, or they would shut up. So we would just sort of pay you under the table. Mostly, I just want you to ask dumb questions to get them started and see what you can figure out. And, I think I could even get the principal to let you out of school for this. He mentioned that you had pretty much finished with school and were bored. Maybe he could count it as credit for 'Social Studies' or something?"

Going along on the sheriff's house calls looking like sort of a little kid who had been whining to go for a ride? Not a very mature image for an almost grown woman, and probably not the sort of way I wanted to be seen by my classmates, but getting an occasional break from school; that was a whole different thing!

"Well, I guess it would be interesting, especially if I could earn a little spending money, and if it was okay with the school, but I am not sure my dad would go with it. Let me talk to him, maybe I can come up with some way to do it."

"Good! You know, a few years ago, your grandma used to help me with things like this, but then, when your grandpa got sick, she kind of lost interest in anything out in the real world."

When we got to the end of the ditch dump road and turned down the lane to my house, the sheriff waved at my dad, plowing the front forty. "Tell you what, Mary, why don't you let me talk to your dad about helping me. I am pretty sure I can get him to come around."

Get my father to come around? Hah! I would never ever again question the authority of the law if he managed to pull that one off!

Chapter 6

DOING SOME SPECIAL WORK FOR THE TOWN

That night after supper, however, Dad called me out to the porch to sit by him on the old swing behind the wisteria vine screen. Out in the yard, the frogs were singing of the coolness of the night air after the heat of the day, and fireflies glowed in the bushes and trees.

"The sheriff told me he was going to give you a little part-time job helping with his bookkeeping entries. Hope you appreciate this. It's a big responsibility for a high school kid. I know you'll do a good job, but I just want you to remember that he is entrusting you with a lot. You know, you can't learn too much of this sort of bookkeeping stuff, and he will give you some real good references. And pay you $1 an hour, too! Now, I want you to plan on saving at least half of what he pays you and putting it in a college fund. No need to go blowing all that on silliness."

He paused, and turned his hands over in his lap. "And, I guess I don't have to tell you, your momma and I are very proud of you."

So, the deal was that I would be going into town with the sheriff every Saturday morning to work with him on his bookkeeping entries, my parents thought, but the reality was that I got to ride along on calls with him to talk to folks having problems getting along with the law.

I actually did help with his bookkeeping, for ten minutes or so a morning, balancing the big town ledger on my lap in the passenger seat by him as we drove on calls, and entering his expenses, money brought in from the town, and fines, in the right columns. My own salary was entered right there, too. When he needed me for special calls, he phoned over to the school, and I would cheerfully abandon my stint in the study hall or the History of Missouri class and go off... "to do some special work for the town". It kept me sane that semester!

Chapter 7

WITCHY WOMAN

The Thursday afternoon that I got to meet old Mrs. Talbot was one of those special calls that the sheriff wanted me on without waiting for our more or less regular Saturday morning visits.

He called the school, and when I walked out down the long sidewalk to the regular bus stop, he was already waiting on the side of the street, with the engine running in the county vehicle, the black station wagon with the nice wood side panels. I hopped in, and threw my History of Missouri book in the back seat through the open grill screen, acting like getting a ride in the official sheriff's car was the most normal thing in the world to me.

"This one is sort of special, Mary", he said. "Mrs. Talbot is a cantankerous kind of lady, to begin with, and getting old hasn't made her any easier to get along with. So, I have been sort of trying to smooth over some complaints I've been getting about her from Old Man Jackson. He runs a bunch of horses out there in a pasture across the road from her orchard, and has been complaining that she's a witch and has been poisoning his horses. Now, 'course, that is a tub of hogwash; there aren't any witches, at least not lately; and..., not in my county, anyway! But he is a real insistent old idiot. Problem is, I know he has connections with those 'Royal Asinine Knights of the Ku Klux Klan'. Now, don't tell your dad I called them that, but they do make my job a real pain in the-well, a real pain..., at times.

"So, we got ourselves a situation. Old Jackson wants me to arrest his neighbor. He claims she hates him and that she has hexed it so that none of his mares ever give live birth. Foals die, and sometimes the mares as well. Then, he gets new lively horses and they run around and are fine for awhile, then die for no reason, except that she has put a spell on them! I told him that is a bunch of swamp-oil, but he's such an ignorant peckerhead! So, I promised to go to talk to her just so he won't decide that he and those stupid white sheet 'riders' should burn a cross on her yard one night ...with her on it!"

It was a pleasant ride out into that part of the country. The land here was hillier than the area where my family had our farm and the sides of the roads were mostly wooded. We were on a hard packed dirt county road that wound along a creek, with large old trees hanging over it. Ferns lined the sides with the occasional gleam of wild flowers tangled in them. Soon we came out to where the road and creek bordered a large rolling pasture dotted with horses. Across the road from the pasture, a mail box set by a small overgrown orchard with apples, shining on the trees and falling in the grass. The little orchard was skirted by a narrow, rutted path that led up a hill into the woods. The sheriff turned the car and headed up a steeper rocky road to a clearing in the trees out of sight from the main road, with a large cabin at the top of the hill. Except for the bird songs echoing in the tall trees, the world was very quiet when the sheriff turned off the engine.

Then everything seemed to explode into a roar of barking and growling as three large black dogs surrounded our vehicle. Their faces were smiling, and their tails wagging fiercely, but their yaps were impressive, and we were hesitant about opening the doors. Stepping out on the running boards seemed to put us in peril of an attack , even if the attack was only a case of wildly overly enthusiastic canine love. Finally, loud screeches from the porch of the house calmed the dogs, and they let us get out and climb up the last of the hill to the cabin, with only an occasional loving nudge from one or the other of our large friendly black escorts.

An old woman in a faded cotton housedress rocked a squeaking rocker on the broad wraparound porch and squinted into the sun at us. The three large black dogs, their job of greeting and warning completed, sat around her feet, panting, with tongue flapping smiles, at us.

She peered at us, then, said with a frown "*Sheriff* Olsen is it? Humph! Pete, I've known you since you were eight years old and stealing my apples."

She glanced at me, still frowning. "Who's this? You have an apprentice apple thief now, Pete?"

"Morning, Mrs. Talbot." The sheriff

sounded hesitant, almost shy. I seemed to catch a glimpse of the eight year old pre-lawman she had caught stealing her apples in the way his hands clutched his hat in front of him, and his shoulders slumped.

"This is Mary Randolph," he continued. "She helps me out part time around the office with the bookkeeping and stuff, and I thought it would do her good to get away from those dusty old files for a little while. You know, it does a kid good to get out into the sun and the outdoors sometimes..." His voice trailed off under the old woman's stare.

She sighed. "Well, Mary Randolph, I may have heard of you. Seems like I've heard that name from Miss Hanson, the librarian. That woman is one of the few folks around here that makes sense to me, and I think she mentioned you in passing. Something about some trouble in town with that weasel they had for a preacher a few years back. Hmph! Well, doesn't matter. My dogs seem to like you, and I guess as long as they do, and you don't steal my apples…, you are welcome here.

"Now, you, Mr. Sheriff with the big badge, what do you want out here today?"

"Look Mrs. Talbot" in a respectful, almost whine, "I know this is crazy, but your neighbor claims that his horses are being poisoned. He thinks it is, well, you know, like witchcraft or something, and I was wondering if you knew anything about it. Not accusing you, you understand, just thought you might be able to give me some information or something…" The sheriff's voice again trailing off to almost a whimper under her hawk-like scowl.

"Pete Olsen! I can't believe you would drive out here on a hot day and ask me something like that!! What hog wallow!

"I wouldn't kill that idiot's horses! I like horses better than most people. And, if those horses aren't smarter than most people, at least they are smarter than that redneck that owns them! But he threatened to shoot my dogs if they barked at his horses. My dogs keep the coyotes away from this hill top, and his meadow, as well as discouraging two-legged predators..., like eight year old apple thieves."

"Yeah, he mentioned he'd had trouble with your dogs barking at him."

"He is a full fledged, card carrying idiot! My dogs are protecting his horses as well as me. He just can't understand that those dogs are doing him a favor! And, Mr. Sheriff Pete Olsen, If he killed my dogs, you better know I would be coming after him, but it wouldn't be with any poison; it would be with my gun!"

Sighing, she continued. "Oh, Pete, you know, those horses are nice critters. When they get over into my apples, I just yell at them and the dogs do bark at them, but then when they leave that is fine with me and the dogs. I wouldn't even think of doing something as sneaky and mean as poisoning them. If you want to figure out what is happening down there, I think you should at least go down and look around that pasture, and not bother me with this silliness!"

The sheriff looked at her for a moment then said, quietly, "Mrs. Talbot, I know you wouldn't hurt those horses. I'll take a little walk down and look around. If you don't mind, I'll leave Mary here in the shade with you, while I do."

Chapter 8

INSIDE THE WITCH'S LAIR

After he left, we sat quietly on the porch. Then, Mrs. Talbot looked over and seemed to notice me for the first time. She saw the bloody scrape on my forearm. "Girl, what did you do?"

"Oh, I just sort of tripped when one of the dogs bumped me. She was just trying to play, and didn't mean to hurt me or anything."

"Well, come out here in the yard with me for a minute, and we'll get something to put on that." She led me down the steps and out around the corner of the house to where the flower beds and wild flowers crowded close to the path. She stopped at a patch of low growing leaves on the ground.

"This plantain is doing real well this year. Here, this will fix that arm right up." Bending, she pulled several broad leaves from some of the plants, then turned and led me back up the steps, across the porch and into the cool dimness of the old wood house.

The inside of the cabin was surprisingly large, with high rough, wooden beams. A big pot-bellied stove was in the center of the lofty main room, with a stack of fire wood in a crate beside the stove. A basket of pine cones for kindling, rested next to the firewood. In the back of the room, I could see stair steps made of split logs that went up to the second floor. Book shelves lined almost all of the walls, with a few strange paintings and old black and white photos tucked in corners on the wall under the stairs. A black leather couch covered with an old quilt was in front of the potbellied stove, with a few old blankets on the floor behind, for the dogs' beds, I guessed. A big wood cook stove was on one side of the room, with a small cloth covered table near. The open rough wood rafters were strung with bundles of various drying plants.

She led me to the rough, crowded counter next to the cook stove, where a rusted, elderly hand pump fed water into the sink.

"Now, we need to just sort of squish these leaves up a little to let the juice soak out. You wash that arm off, while I get a bandage to hold the poultice on."

Humming a little to herself now, she took my cleaned arm and gently spread the more finely chopped leaves on my scrape, then she took a couple of the broad un- -chopped leaves, and laid them over the mashed greens. The last step was to wrap a damp, folded white cotton rag bandage around the arm and tuck the ends of the rag under the rest of the band, so that it would remain in place and tighten when it dried on my arm.

"I think this will do it," she said, looking at her work and smiling for the first time. "There is some yarrow growing over there in the weeds at the edge of the yard, that is good, too, but this was closer, and almost as powerful as the yarrow."

"Now, Mary", her smile was broader and more relaxed now, "I made some special tea this morning and it should be nice and cool by now. Let me get us some and we can just enjoy that on the porch, until your mentor comes back."

The tea, served in oversized ceramic mugs with pictures of castles and rivers on them, was nice and cool, as she had said. It seemed like a mild sassafras brew, but had a lemony taste as well, and was pleasantly sweet. When I told her I liked it, she really broke into a grin. "I brew it myself from the dried young leaves of the sassafras, not the roots. Add some stalks of lemon grass, and sweeten with honey. Now, Mary, you should know to always use honey the bees have made from the flowers around where you live. It will protect you from allergies and all sorts of infections. Besides, it just tastes better!"

She continued, "I see you noticed my mugs. These are some I got in Germany several years ago. I was able to get several. 'Course, they don't all match, as they came from different parts of the country, and some of them are quite old. They are called steins, and are really made to drink beer from, but they are a good big size to have my cold tea in."

"Wow, Germany! You must have got to travel a lot. I saw you had a bunch of neat, strange old books and pictures. Guess it was fun to collect all those things and memories and stuff." Keeping it kind of childish and enthusiastic, to get her ball rolling.

Her grin took on a twinkle, and I wondered if I had laid the childish admiration on a little too heavy, but she continued to beam at me, as she answered. "I did get to travel a lot when I was young, and for the most part, really enjoyed it. But then my parents were getting old, and had health problems so I came back here, settled in, and eventually, got married and had three kids. Really always thought that when I got old here, they would be around some. Sort of envisioned sitting on a big porch kind of like this one, in a rocking chair, kind of like this, but, I thought I would have lots of family and grandchildren that came to see me. Now they all think I don't have any money, and don't bother coming to visit. My fault for raising kids that think that way, I guess."

She shook her head and sighed, "but, as it turns out, I have my three loving, loyal doggie grandchildren, so guess things could be worse. I am lonely more than I would like to be, and some days that sad just eats me, but my dogs are always happy to be with me." Another sigh, then a smile brought her back to the present. "So, I am also really glad that silly sheriff brought you out to visit with me; even if he does want you to figure out if I am a witch?!"

"Oh, I think he knows you aren't a witch. He really likes you, and just doesn't want those stories going around about you." Shifting the subject, carefully now. I had a feeling I was not going to be putting much over on this old lady. "Now I saw a bunch of really strange wood carvings in there. What are those?"

After Mrs. Talbot had taken me inside and showed me the treasures she had gathered in her travels to the outside world, we returned to the porch to await the sheriff.

"I liked all those plants you have

hanging up, too. What are all those for?" Careful not to mention the way that I had heard witches used strange potions.

"Oh, Mary! They aren't for casting evil spells if that's what you are thinking. I study medicinal plants and the herbs that we consider weeds. Some of the things that the Indians used work as well as the gee-gaw medicines you buy in the drugstores, and they are free, and they don't make you sicker than you were before you took them, like a lot of that stuff they use in town."

She paused and drained the last of her tea, setting the empty mug down next to a pair of binoculars on a rough little table by her rocking chair. "It just seems sort of silly to run to town to get something to fix myself with when I have something just as good growing in the woods right here. And a lot of the wild plants out there are okay to eat, too. Since I don't have anyone to take me to the doctor when I get really old, or bring me food, or even care how I am; I better be ready to get by on my own.

"And there are several families of Indian folks around here that have taught me about the plants, and are real friendly and helpful, so they have given me something to look forward to, sort of replacing my family that isn't there. They seem to understand how I feel. Just been a few years since the white folks that came in here and settled, would kill them, and just take their land."

Her face had softened when talking of her Indian friends, but now the frown hovered again. "Besides, I have sort of found a calling in protecting these woods from too many people. These trees are living things, and probably a lot smarter than we humans are. Now, I live up here alone, but when I go to town, I see new houses springing up all along the roads, where there were trees shortly before. People just don't realize how much they are destroying when they sell their woods for money. Once the trees are gone, and folks crowd into those housing developments that use up all the water and shade, the land becomes like dead land..., maybe good for some fancy mowed lawn and landscaping, but that is soon gone. And after the money runs out, and the shoddy houses start to crumble, it is too late to bring the forests and the animals that lived here back.

"So, as long as I have anything to say about it, they don't get to cut my trees. It has got so that I think of the poison ivy, the coyotes, the mosquitoes, the ticks, the snakes, ...and me, a silly old woman that nobody cares about, as the protectors of the woods. As long as we all stand firm and these woods aren't that easy to live in, maybe we can preserve them a little longer. Maybe there will come a day when folks realize that we need areas that are wild and not meant for humans to live in."

She seemed to be getting away from what I wanted to hear about her plants, so I poked her a little. "I did notice that there were some interesting smelling plants drying in there. There's one that smells sort of like wild mint that I can even smell out here. And what are those round bumpy balls you have setting in baskets all around the place? Some sort of fruit, or maybe a big nut of some sort?"

She grinned, the sort of grin that I would expect to see on a kid my age that had a secret to tell. "The 'bumpy balls' are from the Osage Orange tree, but they are not a fruit, or at least not an edible one. The reason I have them setting around is that they keep spiders and bugs out of the house. Really work good, too. Living out here in the woods, in an old log cabin, I would have lots of spiders and bugs without them."

She frowned slightly, then, continued.

"That minty smell is from a wild mint; they call it pennyroyal. The white men had it in Europe, then, when they came to this country they found almost the same plant growing wild here. So they knew how to use it, without even having to check with the Indians. Both the settlers and the Indians knew how to use the oil from the stems and the leaves to make medicine. Now, a lot of folks know you can use it for upset stomach aches, and pneumonia and those other problems that the kids have with breathing sometimes. But it is also good for liver and gallbladder problems. Women can use it to regulate their monthly problems, or as a stimulant. But, the thing that most folks don't know, and it is probably just as well, is that you can use it to get rid of babies who shouldn't be born. The problem with that is that it is so strong, that it often will kill the mothers who are trying to kill their baby, as well as the baby. Now, I wouldn't tell just anybody that, but I am counting on you not being dumb enough to get yourself into the sort of a situation that would lead you to use this stuff. And just as important, I am counting on you not to tell any of those silly girls you know about it. Some things that you know can be just too damned dangerous to share."

Now we could see the sheriff walking up the hill along the dry, dusty path under the trees.

"Guess you'll be going now, Mary. I've enjoyed talking to you. You're not a dummy like a lot of people I meet. And you know how to listen."

"You're real interesting to listen to. Would it be okay if I came back up to visit with you again? You know so much about things I'd like to know more about. I don't drive, so don't know when I could get out here. I have a bike, but the tires flatten out after I ride it awhile. I was thinking maybe I could carry a tire pump with me and fix it, if I needed to, along the way; or maybe I will just have to wait and ride out if the sheriff is coming out this way."

She laughed softly at that, watching the laboring climb the sheriff was making up the hill toward our shady porch retreat. "Anytime would be fine, Mary. I'd be glad of your company, and I suspect the sheriff will be back here before he gets this thing with those dead horses cleared up. I guess something is poisoning them, and since I know it isn't me, I think Mr. Sheriff Pete Olsen would be smart to look around to see who or what it really is instead of listening to that idiot Jackson."

Chapter 9

MORE QUESTIONS THAN ANSWERS

Driving back to the town, the sheriff didn't speak for awhile, but just seemed to need to mull over his findings on the pasture. I was secretly delighted that he didn't even bother to switch the rock and roll radio program off the air, so that I got to enjoy some of the music that my father would have just grimly switched off on our farm. I hung back a secret grin, as I listened to "Blue Suede Shoes". [Knew who was singing that one!] Finally, when "Great Balls of Fire" started to vibrate the car, the sheriff seemed to rouse himself, and after the last "goodness, gracious,~~~!" had rippled the warm air around us in the car, he turned the music off and spoke to me at last.

"Those horses were definitely poisoned. I found the carcass of one that had died a while back. Its legs or at least what was left of the legs after the coyotes got through with it, were drawn up and curled. Poisoned critters go into contortions that pull their limbs up like that. Now, I don't for one minute think Mrs. Talbot would do something like that. She is a tough old bird, but not mean. But did you pick up anything that would make you think she might know something? I don't think she realizes that old Jackson and his buddies might really get worked up and do something to hurt her some night after church."

I had to think about what I wanted to tell him. Mrs. Talbot did seem tough, but underneath her gruff exterior, she seemed to be a lonely old woman. She also seemed a little afraid to admit she was lonely and getting old. I sensed that she hadn't killed the horses, but she might have an idea about why and maybe even how they had died. "I don't think she had anything to do with killing them, either; but maybe since you know the horses were poisoned, you could think of some other person who would have done it. It seems to me, to figure out who did that, you would have to figure out how they did it, then, maybe why they did it would be easier to see."

"How they did it? Well, that's the whole thing of it, isn't it. If somebody poisoned that creek that runs though the pasture, there would be other dead animals around. Jackson said he buys mares that are going to foal, and they seem healthy, but when the colts do come, they are born dead and the mares die having them. He said he has even bought stallions that were bright eyed and running around with their tails standing up, real playful, and had them die within a week. If it was just one horse, I would think maybe a bad snake got it, but when all of them go, it just isn't likely. I sort of looked around for snakes, too, but just saw a couple of king snakes and other harmless critters, but nothing to make me think there were many poisonous dudes around that I wasn't seeing."

The sheriff fumbled in his pocket for the crushed cigarette pack, and shook out a Camel. Holding the steering wheel with one hand, he flicked a large wooden kitchen match across a rough spot on the steering wheel, and lit up.

"Glad you came out with me. Old Mrs. Talbot is pretty lonely, and bitter. Her family has abandoned her, thinking she doesn't have money anymore. You know, Mary, the funny thing is that all those huge old trees out there are worth more than all of them put together will ever make. She loves those woods, and would never let them be cut while she is alive. Meanwhile, every year, they become more and more valuable, so guess that will be a nice big surprise for her heirs..., if she doesn't write them all out of her will and give the whole thing away. She likes those Indian folks who are trying to build a camp ground and a museum and she has talked about leaving them the land to protect it."

He seemed to want some comment from me, so I chimed in. "Guess we have to protect her from her relatives now."

"Uh, yeah, but I have something I need to talk to you about besides this horse poisoning trouble with Mrs. Talbot. And, Mrs. Talbot is really involved in this one, too, come to think of it. You see, there are some girls that go to your school. I think you know them already. Judy, and her sister, Suzie, I've heard you mention. Then, they run around with Betty and Brenda from out close to old Mrs. Talbot's road. I guess you know, the girls' mother committed suicide a couple of days ago. Actually, the mother was Mrs. Talbot's daughter, but there is no real connection with Mrs. Talbot; don't think the family had even visited the old lady in years."

He frowned through his cloud of cigarette smoke at the road ahead. "Well, the thing is, I guess it is suicide, but it doesn't feel right to me."

Clenched jaw around the cigarette stub, "And, Judge Phillips, who is an old time friend of mine, sort of thinks it is questionable, too. The coroner, you know, Dr. Grace, that red headed woman, is not a real people doctor. I mean, not to say she isn't smart and all that, but she is really a veterinarian, and she just took the job of coroner as a favor to the court house. No pay for it, and though she doesn't get many murders, she really doesn't like to study dead bodies and figure out that stuff. Like I said, she is a good animal doctor, but handling dead humans just isn't her real job."

We had pulled up in front of the school by now, and I was going to get out, but he seemed to still want to talk. "Now, I don't really know what I want you to do, but thought you might sort of pal up with those girls and see if anything sounds strange there. Maybe you might want to ride over to the courthouse with me some day, and talk to Dr. Grace. Not that I think she is wrong, you know, but you might come on something there that would make it make more sense for the judge and me. I wouldn't go in with you, but it might be worth our time for you to just sort of ask questions to feel her out."

Now, the sheriff took his cigarette out and frowned at it, then flicked it out the open window. "Okay, just sort of talk to those girls if you can and see if you can fig- ure anything out. I'll talk to you again in a few days."

Chapter 10

PRIMATE MATING RITUALS, CIRCA 1958

The sheriff let me out by the school bus stop, and drove off, seemingly deep in thought. He had left me with some things to think about too.

The girls he had mentioned that he wanted me to get close to were pretty exclusive from the rest of the school. Not the prettiest, or the smartest, they still seemed to have enough bondage in their little group to keep them from wanting to mix with the rest of the high school cliques. They usually stood in a cluster, separate from the rest of the girls, and, as the other girls did, for the most part, ignored the boys. I thought the sheriff had probably forgotten how tight some teenaged groups can be, and how resistant to outsiders when he decided I should infiltrate.

Still musing on this, I found a seat on the cement wall by the road, and watched the other kids milling around waiting for their respective buses. Because our school only had one bus, the driver had to take loads out in all directions, and my ride, out on the gravel ditch dump road was the last one of the day on his rounds. A group of sophomore boys hunched together, sending, under their bushy young-men eyebrows, sideways glances at their female classmates who seemed to be carefully not particularly interested in them. The boys, for the most part, were pretty far along on the maturing thing, but girls their age really just wanted older boyfriends. The ideal catch for a teenaged girl of the time was a boyfriend at least two years older, with a car! The real badge of achievement for a girl of the 50's was a large, flashy boy's class ring hung conspicuously on a chain around her neck. If she chose not to wear it there, but on her finger, there should be a wad of sticky tape bound around it in a clumsy lump that she usually would paint with nail polish on the tape to keep it from smelling bad after getting wet on her hands. A really stylish girl would change that nail polish coat to match her own nails, but sooner of later, the blob of rotting tape beneath those thick built-up coats of nail polish would start to smell too bad and would have to be replaced and the whole process started over.

So, sophomore boys were pretty much not on the female radar yet in high school. They were too young to have a car, or a class ring, and often not possessors of school jackets, let alone a school jacket with a letter blazing on it. They were left, along with their raging hormones and the other boys of their age gang, to gaze at the girls, and, of course, to fantasize and snicker to their compadres.

Although their chances of catching a suitable girl's eye were pretty slim, these boys still clustered in their frustrated herd, replete with greasy ducktail haircuts, motorcycle jackets, but no motorcycle; and the obligatory cigarette pack tucked in a rolled up tee shirt sleeve. I sometimes wondered how many of them actually smoked cigarettes from those displayed trophies, and how many of them just needed the "bad boy" look. By the end of their junior school year, most of the boys also sported leather sleeved school jackets. Of course, the real prizes for their image were those heavy wool "letters" for sports participation that some of them had their moms sew on their jackets or sweaters. I never saw a letter just for getting good grades, music, art, or even for the debate team and I was not sure how many of the letter wearers were good at their sport, or how long it would last in their later post high school years, but for one brief moment they were able to see themselves as young gladiators. Whether the young, desirable girls of the tribe did or not, they seemed to have the hope and maybe even the slight possibility of attracting female companionship.

In these years before the street gangs of the future would adopt their definitive "colors", these young bucks would group together and proclaim themselves in other ways. Chino pants in various colors with a buckle in the back were a favorite tribal statement. The buckling or un-buckling was a statement of their availability, if there had really been girls interested. The crew cuts and ducktail haircuts were held in place, more or less, with heavy globs of Wild Root Cream Oil, or possibly Fitch Rose Hair Dressing oil. When they rode the school buses, they would usually try not to lean their heads on either the windows or the seats of the bus; either way would leave a greasy oil spot when they stood up. Combs would have to be carefully wiped after use because of the glob of goo left on them after the heavy locks were sculpted.

Girls were a little luckier in the hair department. Use of hair spray was a female thing, so French rolls or the new pony tail styles were easier to control. The hair spray of the day worked more or less like a nice coat of lacquer. Of course, some of the romance of that look was ruined if the crisp helmet hairdo was actually touched, but at least there was no drippy grease to contend with. Moments of passion where the hands were run romantically through a perspective mate's hair did not seem to be much of a possibility.

Girls, when not in the classrooms were allowed to wear jeans, clean and neat, with no patches or holes, rolled up half way on the calves above shiny white bobby socks. If you threw on one of your father's white shirts, with the sleeves rolled up and your trophy, bulky, only slightly smelly, taped class ring hanging over a bra that you had stuffed with toilet paper when you left the house, you would be at the top of your game in the "Betty and Veronica" mold of the day.

The real joy of the girls wardrobe, and probably the boys' fantasies, were the full circle skirts over flouncy stacks of net petticoats that held the skirts out at least eighteen inches from the knees, above the white bobby socks in squeaky clean sneakers.

I often found this sort of tribal mating behavior with the preening and posturing, interesting, in the sort of a way that the young bulls and roosters on my dad's farm would strut and lunge to try to impress females while the females would pretend disinterest. This evening, though, I was distracted from the teen scene because I was trying to think of ways to get into the graces of Judy's little group without them becoming too suspicious to open up to me.

Chapter 11

POKING AROUND THE COURT HOUSE

My little espionage assignment from the sheriff of trying to break into that tight group got cut short though, the next afternoon.

I was in the study hall, where I seemed to spend too much of my young life, just getting into a nice open eye dream status; alert enough not to arouse the suspicions of the too-alert study hall teacher, and dreamy enough to try to figure out my strategy for becoming a spy for justice, or at least justice as it was represented by my elderly friend, the sheriff. I was just starting to wonder if getting caught stealing Mrs.

Talbot's apples as a kid had made him a more determined lawman or gave him more understanding of wrongdoers, when my half-awake thoughts were intruded upon by the rubber soled study hall monitor. "The sheriff wants you down at the office?"

It seemed to be understood around the school that I sometimes worked for the town with the sheriff. What I was actually doing and why I was doing whatever it was, seemed to be a matter of conjecture by the teachers and some of the other students. I wasn't that noticeable or important enough to normally warrant a lot of gossip, but there seemed to be a rising little idle curiosity about what was going on with my sudden exits from the school in the company of our aging sheriff. The principal, of course, could have let them in on what was going on, but he seemed to get a great deal of amusement in carefully watching me from afar, after my rather vague trip at the start of the school year with my great uncle, Perry Moonwalker.

"Mary, I want you to come with me over to the court house." Again, when I got to the back parking lot door of the school, the sheriff was waiting in the dusty county car with the motor chugging. "I'm not happy about this explanation that this lady supposedly committed suicide a few days ago, and think I need to talk to the vet-uh- the coroner, again. Thought you might come in handy to go along and listen to her, and see what you think."

He threw the stick shift into gear and roared out of the school parking lot, turning onto the street with squealing tires. Frowning, "Now, I am going to take another look at the body too, but you can skip that. 'Know a young girl doesn't need that sort of experience."

Not take a look at the body?! Fat

chance of that, Mr. Sheriff man!

"Oh, I'll be okay. I've always watched my folks butcher on the farm, you know. Don't think a dead lady will be too scary."

He seemed to relax at that. "Good! Not sure what good it will do, but you're pretty good at picking up on stuff."

When we pulled up and parked under the shady old trees surrounding the Benton court house, the sheriff glanced at his watch.

"It isn't quite time for the judge to recess his court for lunch yet. We might as well go on over to the coroner's office and get that over with. We can catch old Harland when we get done there."

Chapter 12

LADY CORONER

Cutting across the old cobblestone side street, we entered the small office marked in big gold letters "Grace Prescott, D.V.M, Veterinarian," and the office hours painted across the glass door, with a small hand lettered sign stating quietly, almost embarrassedly, it seemed to me, "County Coroner". A cardboard sign with a clock hung in the window with a "closed, back in 20 minutes" sign on it. The sheriff ignored the sign and walked in. Guess he thought that badge was a ticket into anywhere.

The lady that was sitting at the desk in the little office when we walked in was obviously on her lunch break. Bare feet propped on the desk, in nylon stockings with one run in them, white professional coat hung on the back of a chair, she sat with a Woman's Day magazine in one hand, and a sloppy wax paper wrapped sandwich in the other.

She was sort of well developed in the way that I thought men were interested in; the way I always thought of that actress, Miss Marilyn Monroe, as being. Very fierce red hair with gold wisps at the sides framed her face, and she reminded me a bit of the pretty nude ladies I had seen painted by those old Europeans in the books. Pretty or not, her face was also a little fierce at the moment, as she looked up from her bologna and white bread sandwich to frown at our intrusion on her break. "That sign on the door reads 'Closed', Sheriff, if you can't read it!"

"Hi, Doc. I thought it would be a good idea to get in to see you while you didn't have any customers to see. And this is official county business, anyway."

Putting her feet down on the floor into sensible oxford type shoes, and pulling on her white medical jacket, she sighed. "Okay, Sheriff, should have known it was too quiet to last." She glanced toward a covered dish sitting on her desk. "One of my customers, she has dogs, not dead bodies, brought me in a banana cream pie. If you would like some, there is plenty for all of us."

A few minutes later, with the pie cut and pieces served on the hard plastic dishes that were stored in the back of the file cabinet, she seemed to look at me for the first time and smiled. "And who is this?"

"This is Mary Randolph. She kind of works for my office; you know, does book work and such. I just brought her along for the ride. Need to talk to you some more about that dead lady, and take a look at the body again."

"Sheriff, I took this job as a favor to the county, not as a detective or something! I can tell you what I see, but it isn't really my job to be trying to solve your crimes, and I don't like having to trot that poor dead lady out for every wandering guy that comes in off the street, sheriff or not! You ought to tell that judge of yours to sign off on her and let me give her family the remains. They deserve to get to take her home. Besides, my cooler isn't really geared for keeping human bodies in. I am just a vet, you know."

"Oh, yes ma'am. I know all that, and I am going to talk to Judge Phillips in a few minutes, and by golly, I will remind him of that."

The coroner, at least for while we were there, she was the coroner, was not pleased when I trotted along into the examination room where she was keeping the body. But I had brought a clipboard from the back seat of the sheriff's car, with my old shorthand notebook clipped to it, and poked a pencil behind my ear, and had another one in my hand, looking all the world, I thought, like a real investigative secretary. I also made a point of not making eye contact as she led us back, and uncovered the poor body.

I was pretty cool, and determined to be professional, as I knew the sheriff did not like to deal with this part of his job. But, the first look at the body gave me slight pangs of nausea, fear and disgust, followed shortly after with a huge sense of loss and regret for the woman who had lived in this body and was now forever gone. Her husk was totally dead and stiff, drained it seemed by death of all color, except a sad grey tone. I had learned to see colors around live people that gave me some clue as to who they were inside, but this poor body had no clue of the life and personality of the person who had lived in it.

"She wasn't found for several days, and as she was already drawn into a ball like that, and stiffened up, I just left her like that until they get ready to bury her."

Dr. Prescott glanced at me, and when she spoke again, seemed to be directing herself at me more than the sheriff, who was trying to look over the body at some framed certificates on the wall. "You see that half her head was blown away. Not a lot of blood, which is strange, but like I said it was several days and the blood probably evaporated and flaked away when they brought her in. She was holding the shot gun between her knees, I guess. She didn't leave a note, but sometimes folks don't when they get so sad they think they have to die. So, like I said, it seems like a suicide. Pretty cut and dried. 'Course, you know, I am just really a vet, not a people doctor, but that is the way I see it."

"You can cover her back up now, Doc." the sheriff said, still not really looking at the grey husk curled on the table. "I'm going over to talk to the judge now. And I'll tell him you want to get the body out of here. Guess there is really no reason to keep it in your way."

 # Chapter 13

HERE COMES THE JUDGE

Of course, it seemed like I had heard of the famous Judge, Harland Phillips all my life, so I was pretty excited about getting to meet him; but the man who was pulling off his robe and hanging it in the closet in his office was a surprise. He seemed in many ways to be like a boy, not too many years older than I was, but he covered that boy inside of his brain carefully with a fierce, hawk like demeanor. Tall and skinny, "lanky" was the word that came to mind, he seemed to fold himself into the imposing chair behind his judicial desk.

He probably didn't mean for me to get a glimpse of the gun that he wore in a waist holster on his belt behind his back, but that also gave me a clue toward how he thought.

"So, this is Miss Mary Randolph. I've heard about you, young lady, and am glad you are helping out our county sheriff here. Hope you are learning a lot from him." He extended a bony, long-fingered hand to me.

Learning a lot?! Seems like I am the one doing the teaching. What is it about men that they always have to twist things around so they are the natural born leaders?

"Yes sir." Big, stupid, pumpkin grin. No need in saying much until I figured him out.

"Harland, we've just been over to Dr. Prescott's office. She says it is pretty cut and dried as a suicide and we should just release the body for the family to bury. Poor folks have been through so much already."

"She says that does she? Sheriff, I tell you, it just doesn't feel right to me. She was going through a real fight divorcing her husband and fighting him and his family. She was trying to get half of the family business and all the other stuff that the family had. Pretty sure the company would have to be sold, probably real cheap, for her to get all she asked for; but she was going to do it. A woman that mad and determined doesn't sound to me like a woman who would just give up and quit. And not leaving a note heaping a ton of blame on their heads for driving her to it?! Not likely, I think."

His eye dropped on me after this outburst, "And what do you think, Missy? The sheriff tells me that you are good at figuring stuff out. What's your take on this?" He almost snarled. "Come on, impress me!"

"Maybe you should go talk to Dr. Grace yourself. You know she likes to help people and would like to do the right thing for the woman's family. But maybe, she should just look at that body like she would a dead animal, and see what she would think about the body if it wasn't a real woman there. She seems to be sort of feeling too bad because she was looking at a poor dead human lady and not thinking of it as just dead meat."

The judge let out a cackle at that. "Dead meat!" Shaking his head, still chuckling, "You farm girls are a real hoot sometimes, but maybe you're right. Maybe she does need to look closer. 'Course, she is a real spitfire when she gets mad, so maybe I should just walk over there myself this afternoon. Got a case that should tie up early, then, am probably going to be able to call it a day early enough to catch her before she leaves the office."

 # Chapter 14

Sidebar — with Asparagus...

Harland had had other encounters with the coroner in the past that had not gone well. She had, on several occasions, whined at him for having to do the free job for the county in handling the few questionable deaths that came in. She felt that she was not really trained to handle dead humans, and besides, he suspected, she seemed to be a little disgusted by human corpses.

He had gotten angry and yelled at her the last time they had talked. Sort of thought she was a little, well, maybe a little too belligerent and practically ordered her out of his office; but this current death had him thinking it was time to make peace with her and get the job at hand taken care of before he got mad at her again.

Besides, the county couldn't afford to hire a real coroner.

So, after his last case had closed for the evening, he carefully hung up his robe, and slipped on the spare shirt he kept in the closet of his office, and combed his hair neatly into place. After he checked his hair in the mirror, he turned and twisted to see that his loose shirt successfully covered the small hand gun he wore in a holster in the small of his back. *No need going over to have a civilized conversation with that ditzy red-headed vet/coroner with his concealed gun unconcealed!*

Then, going out the back door of the almost deserted, quitting-time court house, he lingered in the vacant over grown lot be-hind the building, and gathered what he thought would be a few tools to placate the lady coroner.

His timing was good, and he walked into the coroner's office just as she was hanging up her official lab coat. He was carrying a huge bouquet of wild daisies, Queen Anne's lace and wild asparagus spears and, opening the door to the office without knocking, he smiled his glibbest, most peace-making smile, not an easy task for him. It used facial muscles that he worked all day, every day, to suppress during his normal line of work on the bench.

"Hi. I think we sort of got off on the wrong foot in the past, and felt like we should be on better grounds to work on this case." He kept the smile pasted on in the face of the scowling red-head, and in spite of the overpowering smell of that banana cream pie still sitting on her filing cabinet.

"Judge, what are these!?"

"Well, you don't seem like the sort of woman who would want anything too frilly, but these daisies and the Queen Anne's lace are just crowding out everything on the hill behind my court house. Needed pruning anyway, and the asparagus is just really going wild this year, too; so thought I would just bring you some for your supper."

She didn't seem to be responding to his attempted gallantry, so he continued "And I wanted to talk to you about holding on to the dead woman in your lab. We really need you to check her again. Know it was a gunshot, but..."

"Harland, I just took this stupid job as a favor to the county. I am not a coroner; and have no desire to be one. I am a vet, pure and simple. I take care of animals and that is what I want to do. I do this thing for your court without pay, and do the best I can, but I am NOT a coroner!" There was not really steam coming from her nose as she spoke, but Harland could see her rather cute little jaw tightening into a dangerous clamp over her growing irritation.

"Well, Madam, I understand all that, but as one officer of the court to another, I must officially ask you to give this matter your further consideration."

"OK, then, Harland,-uhh, your Honor, if it is an official request, I'll go over the body one more time."

The Coroner bit her lip, then picked up one of the plump green asparagus spears and turned it over in her hands, thoughtfully. "But, you know, Harland, if I didn't know better, I would suspect you were bringing me some sort of a male phallic symbol offering here."

Harland turned and left her office, slamming the door. *The nerve of that woman, talking that way to a judge! Plump, red-headed and feisty! And she's no spring chicken, either; should have enough sense to know not to talk that way to a judge!*

But as he stepped into the hall, Harland was surprised to feel a blush rising to stain his weathered face, and even more surprised to feel a laugh welling up inside his chest. It had been a long time since a woman made him laugh!

 **Chapter 15**

A SHARE OF
THE PRETTIES

After supper that night, I had planned to try to ask my dad a few questions, but before I could think out how to approach him, he called me out to sit on the porch with him and he had a few questions of his own.

"Now, how's your job with the sheriff coming? I heard some men at the hardware store talking about this woman who killed herself out there west of town. Have you heard your boss say anything about that? Sounds a little strange to me."

"Yes, I think he has some questions about her, himself. I think I heard she was getting divorced from her husband and was going to get half the business. 'Course, I don't really know too much, but it sort of seems like there is more to that than is coming out."

My mom had left her after-supper quilting, and had come out to settle on the old porch rocker to listen to us. Now, she spoke quietly in the dark. "Mary, you know, we know you do other stuff for the sheriff besides 'bookkeeping'. We trust that he is too much of a gentleman, and too old, to try to take advantage of a girl like you, but we know there is more to that job then you have told us. Now, don't insult our intelligence by acting too 'dumb'."

"Besides," my father added, "I saw you riding in the sheriff's official car over by the courthouse the other day."

I was glad that we were sitting in the dim light now, as I could feel an embarrassed heat rising to my face. I knew I was supposed to keep quiet about what I was doing for the sheriff, and assumed that I could easily fool my parents, but evidently I wasn't as good at this subterfuge thing as I thought.

"Well, he takes me along with him when he talks to folks. He thinks that having a kid along makes them let their guard down. And sometimes I can figure out things that they don't want to tell him."

"Yeah, you always were a nosey kid", Dad said. "We aren't too worried about you snooping around things for him. That is probably what you are best at; just wanted to keep track of what you were doing."

"So, what were you doing at the courthouse?" My mom didn't often talk a lot, but this thing probably smelled too interesting to just let go.

"Well, we went over and talked to the coroner about that dead woman. Dr. Grace is real nice, but she doesn't like that job. Says all she really is supposed to be is a veterinarian, but she does these jobs for the county when she has to. Doesn't get paid for the coroner stuff, either."

No need to mention seeing the corpse to my parents. That might make them get a little uptight.

"And that is all?"

Damned! My mother was pretty good at sniffing out stuff, herself.

"Well, then, we did go across the street and meet the judge."

"You met the judge!?" My dad was obviously impressed, now. "I've heard he is a real straight shooter."

A straight shooter? I wondered what my dad would think if I told him that not only was the judge a "real straight shooter" but that he carried that cute, mean-looking little gun under his robe in the court.

"Yeah, he seemed nice." "Nice" was a word I always used with my parents when I wanted to throw up a little smokescreen over what I really thought. Now I was wondering if they ever figured me out on that one as well. "He and the sheriff are wondering if that woman that died was really a suicide or not. The vet says she was, and wants to just let her family have the funeral, but the sheriff and the judge are wanting to know more."

"So she was trying to get a divorce and take half the family trucking business. Well, that is real bad news for the family. Not just the husband, but the whole family. It has been in his family for at least four generations that I know of. His grandpa, or maybe his great grandpa, don't really remember which one it was, started that out in the twenties, using his old farm truck to drive his neighbors' crops to the market. That family seems real rich in comparison to most of the folks around here, but things will change for their kids now. You know, those daughters of his live the sort of lifestyle I would like to see you girls living someday, but I doubt if it will ever happen."

Dad paused and took a sip of his fruit jar of iced tea, and continued. "See, Mary, what happens when a big family business like that, even one where there seems to be lots of money, gets divided up, is that it affects everybody in the family. He would have to sell at least part of the trucks and warehouses to even give her half of what it is worth. And, if the business is under a cloud like that, even old customers won't give them contracts. No use signing a trucking contract when the trucks may get sold out from under, and the business dissolves. And the banks will drop them real fast, instead of giving loans to get him over the rough times. Now, I don't know what went on between them, maybe she should get half of everything, but this is what her husband has known all his life. He started driving local deliveries when he was sixteen, and went on to do the interstate stuff before he took on the whole business from his dad and granddad. So, it is all he really knows how to do, and all he really wants to do. Now, for whatever reason, he will be the generation to sell that big rich company that his family built for all those years. It will be gone, and his marriage will be gone, and in many ways, all of his family will be gone, too."

The silence that stretched after Dad's voice died was sad and empty. Finally, not being able to stand the hopelessness that seemed to have sunk over my parents, with the wisdom of my maturing years, I said "Gee. Maybe she should have just had a mad passionate affair and stayed married."

Momma seemed to choke on that one, while I could feel the heat of Dad's glare in the dark. "Don't talk dirty young lady! What trashy novels have you been reading now?"

"But why would she kill herself when she was taking on such a fight?" My momma was good at getting to the nut of the problem, while Dad fussed around about the husband losing his family business part of the situation.

He shook his head in disgust and continued, "I heard she expected part of his grandmother's jewelry when she died, but it was held in a trust for her two daughters. And, she had worked with the rest of the family in the office for over twenty years, so maybe there were two sides to the story that we don't hear."

"But wanting a share of the pretties is not an excuse to kill yourself." My mom was usually quiet in these discussions, but this one seemed to bother her. "Her mother, Mrs. Talbot, that friend of yours, Mary, is heartbroken over the whole thing, the mailman told me, and she is worried about her granddaughters having to do without now.

The mailman said that they never write her, not even 'thank-you notes' but she sends them cards with checks in them in the mail every birthday and Christmas. He is not real sure how big all of those checks were, ...said some of the envelopes were too thick to really make the amounts out real clear, but said that what he could make out on those checks seemed like a lot of money to be giving family who don't even bother to come see you."

Chapter 16

QUESTIONS THAT LEAD TO MORE QUESTIONS

The next morning, on the bouncy road to school I used the back of the quiet, dusty bus as a place for meditation. Somewhere in the back of my mind, there seemed to be a connection with the poisoned horses and the woman who died by a gunshot wound that the judge and the sheriff didn't think was self inflicted.

The obvious answer to these almost unrelated incidents would be my friend, old Mrs. Talbot. She lived alone out there in the woods; and wasn't friendly with the folks around her *Except for the Indians. Could this be Indian witch doctor magic? Somehow, even I couldn't make that connection.*

She had long conversations with her dogs and studied and knew plants. In another age, she would be a perfect candidate to be burned under the title of "Witch", but the twentieth century was a little too sophisticated for that. ...Weren't we?

And, would she have shot her daughter to save the family business and provide for her granddaughters? I knew, although she never spoke of them, except to say that she was disappointed in not seeing them much, that she missed them and cared for their welfare. As I remembered, there were numerous black and white photos on her cabin walls of the girls at different stages of their lives. According to my momma, the postman had even inspected her mail and told Momma, and probably most of the folks on his route, that she sent them a good deal of money gifts. Of course, I wasn't sure what a "good deal of money" meant, probably different things to the different folks that stopped to listen to him.

I was pretty sure she wouldn't hesitate at killing someone who threatened the welfare of her family, even a daughter, but I also knew she would only do it as a last resort.

So that line of thought seemed to lead me back to the dead horses. What could cause apparently healthy, even frisky horses that were in great spirits one day, galloping around their green beautiful pasture, to be lying drawn up in tight crumpled, twisted shapes of death the next day? And, what is the connection here that I am still not seeing? Maybe I should make an excuse to go talk to the vet about animal deaths as well as her human corpse.

By the time I got to the end of the ride, and lurched to the front of the bus to get off, I still hadn't come up with answers, but had decided that my next steps should be to get into the minds of Mrs. Talbot's granddaughters, and their little clique, and talk the sheriff into giving me a ride to the courthouse coroner's office.

Chapter 17

FIELD TRIP WITH THE VET

As it turned out, I didn't have to persuade the sheriff to give me a ride after all. In the middle of the Missouri history class [we were up to Lewis and Clarke; pretty hard to make that part boring, but...] a runner from the office came up to the classroom with a message that I was wanted in the office. When I got downstairs, though, I found that it was not the sheriff's familiar shambling bulk waiting for me as I expected, but a woman with a mane of blazing red hair forming a torch like halo around her face, standing in the diffused light from the frosted glass door of the office.

"Mary, I am going out to take a look at those poisoned horses for the sheriff, and he suggested that I take you along. Said he didn't think you would mind getting out of school for a couple of hours."

Mind? I figured I could always catch up with Lewis and Clark later. They may have been great explorers, but they were long dead and would still be there when I got back to them.

When we got to the wild pasture, we didn't go up the hill to Mrs. Talbot's cabin, though I suspected she knew we were there. Her dogs were barking that we were down at the bottom, but didn't come running down to investigate, so I figured she had kept them closed in the cabin while we were there. Somehow, I felt that she would be sitting in that old rocker of hers watching us with those binoculars that she kept on the porch table.

Dr. Grace paused before getting out,

after she parked her jeep. Then, she reached up and untied the scarf that had, rather unsuccessfully, kept that flaming red hair pulled back, and shook her head vigorously. "Mosquitoes are going to be bad out there, Mary. You might want to have your hair around the back of your neck as much as you can. They will still come after us, but might as well cover up as much as possible to sort of slow down their lunch."

So, with my hair shook into a wild tangle and wearing an extra long sleeved work shirt that the vet had thrown in the back of the jeep with her own, we set out to inspect the dead animals and their pasture.

The pasture was in the full rich bloom that I would have expected at this time of the year. Blooming wild flowers tangled in the grasses, with the soft blues of the chicory blooms crowding the golden glow of the Black-Eyed-Susans, and the softly wind-tossed beauty of those white lace parlor doilies, the Queen-Anne's-Lace. A few pre-blooming goldenrod, and the royal purple iron weed were there, and seemed to be waiting for the first crisp of fall to hit them, to burst into their own exuberant show against the future red and gold leaves that would appear in a few weeks. The rich dark smell of the wild mint in the marsh fogged my nostrils and reminded me of the healing powers of the pennyroyal that Mrs. Talbot had described. Here, the low marshy mead-ow ground was bisected about in half by a meandering, shallow creek, and trees sur-rounded the whole area, making a shady fringe. All was a real delight, until I realized that with the visual impact, and the fra-grance of the swamp, I was also listening to the whine of the mosquitoes that Dr. Grace had predicted would greet us there.

As we waded around through the marshy pasture, I noticed that Dr. Grace was paying particular attention to the plants growing low on the ground, and even stopped on a couple of a occasions to pull a few dead leaves off of the ground cover by the creek. The creek seemed to cut down from around a cornfield next to the pasture, but on higher ground to this lower, wetter ground. This lower wet area was probably too wet to raise field crops but served well for growing hay and pasturing horses.

Finally in the bushes around the fence, she found what she seemed to be looking for, the rotting carcass of a very small, young colt. It's head had been detached and taken away by predators, but the skeleton was still pretty intact. Most of the shredded muscles and some of the ragged hide were still in place, though the guts seemed to have vanished. The limbs were tightly twisted and drawn up to the body

"Okay, Mary. What we are looking at here is a poisoned horse. I think it is probably an arsenic poisoning. Going to take samples of the body, the mud around the creek, and some of the foliage from around the creek that the horses have been eating. And, are those old trees across the road apple trees?"

She had nodded toward the trees that I knew were Mrs. Talbot's so I was able to answer with assured knowledge, "Yes, Ma'am. Those are the apple trees that the horses were getting out to eat the fruit from. That is why the sheriff and I had to come out here awhile back. Mr. Jackson was claiming she was a witch."

She paused from her work of cutting samples from the dead animal now, and straightened, rubbing the small of her back. "Yeah, I heard about that. Just like the forbidden fruit from the Bible, huh? Well, those trees might have a little something to do with these dead horses after all; apple seeds are poisonous to horses in large amounts. But I think this might just be a case where several things worked together to poison these animals. I want to take these samples back and check on some things before we really can say what happened here."

Going back into town, the vet turned on the radio and hummed along with the rock and roll station. She seemed to be purposely avoiding conversation.

Finally, she spoke. "There is another thing about those horses. Horse traders used to give small amounts of arsenic to horses they were trying to make look and act younger. They would sell the horses that were suddenly lively and bright-eyed to unsuspecting farmers and be long gone by the time the frisky, bright-eyed horses would suddenly drop dead from arsenic poisoning. Thought they sort of cracked down on those dealers in this part of the country several years ago, but there could be somebody out there still pulling this sort of a scam."

I had been thinking about a different sort of problem, and was thinking of how to get her interest, when I knew she was tired of the whole "dead lady in the examination room" problem. "It seemed sort of funny to me how that the woman with the shot off head was curled up like those dead horses. I wonder how she could hold that big old shot gun if she was that twisted up before she died."

"O, Mary, I don't know. Dead bodies do strange things. I think that the sheriff and that judge just look for things that aren't there."

She was clearly getting annoyed now, so I contented myself with dropping my questions; sometimes when the hook is set, you just have to let the fish chew the bait.

Now, I just settled into being the slightly silly teenager that she expected me to be, humming along with the music by that great new *sexy?!* singer - that used to be my friend, Sonny. The liquid notes of his recording of "Don't be Cruel" echoed in my head for the rest of the drive back to the school.

Chapter 18

A MIRACLE SPRAY

I had plenty to ponder that night while I helped with the farm chores, and getting food on the table, as well as worked afterward with my tired mother, cleaning up the kitchen until the next onslaught of feeding the family. After I dried the dishes and put them away, and wiped the round oak table that served as the work area and dining table in the hot little kitchen, I decided to try to talk some things out with my dad.

"I guess you know I'm helping the sheriff look at those poisoned horses out there west of town? Well, he hasn't quite figured out how it happened yet, and I was wondering if you might have any ideas on how I could help him with that?" Keep it easy and super respectful; that always seemed to get him into a mood to tell me stuff when I wanted some information from him..., which wasn't often, of course.

"Does he know what kind of poison they were killed with?

"No, the vet is testing some samples from around the area. Think she sort of thinks it is arsenic or something like that. Or maybe just a combination of stuff that sort of added up to kill them. Doesn't matter much as I can see, they are dead, and that is the bottom line. They just need to know what from so that they can figure out if someone did it, or what."

"Yeah, I can understand that, and you might be right in thinking it was a combination of stuff that did it." He took a sip of his tea in the dark. "I always sort of worried about poisons getting to our animals and crops, too. You know they brought out that

DDT right about the time the war was getting over; everyone thought it was going to be a real miracle spray. I used it a lot here in this house when we first moved in. So damned hot and steamy, we had to have all the windows and doors open. But most of those old screens had holes in them; some just from pure old age rusting them out. Anyway, I sprayed a lot of the 'miracle spray' around the place those first couple of years. Of course, they said it wouldn't hurt people, but after awhile, I got to wondering about that. You remember how all our barn cats got sick and died when we first came here. We thought there was some sort of disease they were catching. Remember how they would be okay for awhile, then we'd see them sitting in the sun out on the rocks behind the barn, shaking and shivering until they died. Well, it just seemed strange to me. We'd never call the vet for just a barn cat, but you hated to see them die, anyway.

So, I got to thinking about it. How the DDT was killing the flies and bugs. The barn swallows ate the flies and bugs, and the cats ate the birds. So, all that poison was just going up the line to the cats. Probably every poisoned bird just added that much more poison to what the cats were storing in their bodies already, until it killed them. And, of course, I couldn't help wondering what it was going to do to people when our bodies stored enough of this poison; really bad stuff... So, these guys that are doing stuff to the crop seeds now sort of make me think of all those dead barn cats. I know they claim you'll make more money off their treated seeds, and that it won't really hurt anyone, but I also think some of those guys would kill off their grandma if the price was right. So, I'm just not going to do it."

He laughed then, an unexpected chuckle in the dimness, then, shook his head.

"So I guess your old Dad will never get rich as a farmer."

Probably because this wasn't the way he usually talked to me, I had a rare vision of him as a person, rather than a parent. When I found myself looking at him without the barriers of his role as my parent, I saw a frustrated, but hard working, and honestly stubborn man. Becoming aware of the aura that my father wore around himself was surprising. I seemed to be able to see things about other people, but my own parents were just too close and powerful for me to see the people they were underneath.

"No, Dad, you may never have a lot of money, but you'll be rich in other ways."

Dad looked at me sharply in the dusk. Finally he spoke with a touch of softness that I was unaccustomed to, under his gruffness.

"Uhh. Well, I think you better go finish helping your Mom with those dishes."

Chapter 19

THE BODY
IN THE SUITCASE

Despite my father's doubts, I was by no means convinced that the big seed companies or that company that was starting to develop those chemicals that would let the farmers grow bigger crops and kill off the pests and weeds would put out a product that would hurt humans. After all, that company was from St. Louis, our own Missouri city just up the road and the home of our beloved Cardinals baseball team. *Please, give me a break, Dad!* Everyone knew our government would never let something like that happen, anyway.

But, putting the thought of dead horses, and dead cats aside, I decided that today I would work on getting close to that strange little clique of girls the sheriff wanted to know more about.

So, the next morning after my talk with Dad, I threw an aside over my shoulder to my parents as I walked out to catch the bus. "I need to go over to Judy's house there in town after school, if it is okay. There is a Future Farmer's Barn dance in the gym tonight, and my principal said I should go. There will be food there, and if Dad could pick me up afterwards, about eight-thirty, I can get a ride to it with Judy and her sister."

My dad didn't look too pleased with the idea of having to drive into town at night, but had to accept it if the principal said it was something I should attend.

The next step of my plan was a little more complicated. After the fourth period bell rang and we trooped to the next class, I managed to get up next to Judy in the hall, and gave my widest, most confident grin as I said "Remember how you wanted me to visit your house some evening? I was thinking I could go over to your place with you after school and then go to the barn dance from there. My dad is going to pick me up, but I thought this would give us a nice time to get better acquainted."

Still smiling in the face of her wide-eyed blank, I pulled out the big guns. "And you could tell me more about this dance in Memphis. I probably couldn't really go, but it does sort of sound interesting."

"Oh, Mary, com'on. Let's skip the last period. It is sooo boring in that class, and they probably won't notice we are gone, anyway."

So, after hiding in the bathroom until the halls were clear, and carefully letting ourselves out the janitor's back door, we trooped through the field behind the school and back onto the old sidewalks of the town.

"I know the druggist real well. Let's stop there and get a cherry vanilla cone."

"I don't have any money."

"That is okay; he and my mom are real good friends and he always slips me one for free."

"He really likes my mother's music, and he is real friendly to my sister and me, too."

I had heard about the druggist from the gossip around town. He was a Jewish man who had come west to set up a business several years before. He had built a beautiful brick home that impressed the folks in town, and then, because there were no other Jewish folks around, he married a nice Catholic woman. They seemed to be pretty happy, having parties in their home, and hosting musical recitals by Judy's mom and other local musicians. Then, after they had been married awhile, the druggist's wife had a baby, and it must have been a bad birth, as his wife died a few days later. The baby boy lived a little while after they buried his mother in the Catholic cemetery, but despite the fancy supplements and things that the druggist used to try to make him strong, the baby, too, died.

After the baby died, folks noticed that the drug store was shut down for a couple of weeks with only a "closed" sign on the door, and no explanation.

Everyone wondered if the only drug store in Southeast Missouri at the time was going to be permanently closed by the bereaved husband and father; but he suddenly turned up one morning with the store doors open, polishing the brass railing around the oiled wood soda counter, seemingly conducting business as usual.

Later, Mrs. Mason's traveling train-conductor husband, on one of his rare visits home, explained that the Jewish man had gone on one last mission for his son. He had taken the sad little body up to St. Louis on the train to a place where there were enough other Jewish folks to conduct a proper Jewish burial and mourning service for the baby boy.

Mr. Mason claimed that he had even helped the quiet, sad man put the little body in the suitcase on the luggage rack where the father could watch it for the five hour train ride to the St. Louis Grand Central Station.

Chapter 20

CHERRY VANILLA WITCHCRAFT

The drug store was in an old long narrow brick building, with fancy tile floors, and pretty inlaid colored glass windows on either side of the big brass door with the bell. Down one side of the store, ran a long counter with all the mysterious drug items on the wall behind the counter. On the other side of the store, toward the back, a soda fountain bar ran with the mirrors behind the counter reflecting the colored shards of light and bouncing it off the polished brass. There was a glow on the wood and on the shiny leather seats of the high bar stools inwardly facing the soda ice cream center. The whole place smelled of lemony wood polish, ancient wood, and a sort of vanilla ice cream mix smell.

I was a little embarrassed to be there with Judy for the express purpose of pan-handling an ice cream cone off the druggist; but Judy seemed to have no qualms about asking for the treat, grinning and sparkling at him as she introduced me to him as her "very best friend in the whole world, except for you, Mr. Huffman". Her performance seemed the ultimate in tacky to me, but it must have charmed Mr. Huffman, because he didn't even wait for her request, but dipped up two beautiful cones of the cherry vanilla ice cream, a creamy smooth ice cream rich with whole halves of exotic maraschino cherries. The goodness of the ice cream went a long way toward making me feel less than guilty about the freeload-ing.

While we ate our cones, perched on the high bar stools, Mr. Huffman leaned on the glass case and beamed at us. He was a rather small man, with thin, wispy blonde hair, and very large, surprisingly beautiful blue eyes behind the thick lenses of his glasses. "So, Miss Judy, how is your family these days. Is your mom still playing? I haven't seen any of her concerts being advertised in the paper lately. I certainly hope she is still doing her music."

"O yes, she is doing a lot of work with that new music teacher from the high school. And, you know, my dad is still sick. She is gone a lot at night, so my sister and I take turns staying with him. He takes a lot of fussing over, but lately, I have been going on so many dates, and things that poor Suzie has had to spend most of her evenings with him. 'Course, she just doesn't have all the social obligations that I do." Slight toss of her head. "And dates! Did I mention dates?"

Watching Judy's pretentious performance, I felt with regret, even the richness of the jewel-like cherries becoming a little cloying in my mouth. Mr. Huffman seemed to be totally impressed by her little scenario though, and continued to beam at her behind his thick glittering glasses.

"Oh, yes. And you know, I don't ever go out with those greasy haired boys. Give me one of the guys with the crew cuts and the buttoned down shirts every time. I know I can control them. Yes, sir! No surprises from them. They know they have to do what I say!"

The polished bell on the front door tinkled an interruption to Judy's well-spun stories, and the slight figure of her younger sister, Suzie, was framed in the sunlight from the opened door. Her arms were loaded with a huge fluff of freshly cut flowers, and though, as usual, she didn't make eye contact with any of us, she proudly carried them up to the druggist.

"Here are those flowers I promised you, Mr. Huffman. I picked some for my mom, too, and wanted to bring these over before they wilt."

Mr. Huffman, obviously pleased with this teenage invasion of his normally rather sterile drugstore domain, pulled an old white oversized vase from below his cash register and hurried over.

"I'll just put these in water, then, set them in the showcase in the window." He beamed at the fluffy blue hydrangeas and the lacy white blooms that Suzie had brought in.

Then, still beaming shyly, he said, "Suzie, you need to go back in the back and wash your hands and arms really good. Use that heavy duty soap on them. I know it stings, but you need to get really clean. Then, come up front with your sister and her friend, and I think I can find an ice cream cone with your name on it."

When Suzie came back to join us, the druggist smiled fondly at her rough red skinned hands and arms and presented her a cherry vanilla ice cream cone with a flourish.

Something about this whole thing was bothering me, so I had to ask. "Why did you make her wash up so good? All she had really done was pick flowers for you."

He busied himself rubbing the soda fountain counter to a higher degree of shiny. Then, not looking up, "Well, Mary, all those 'flowers' she brought in are extremely toxic. Those hydrangeas can cause folks to get really sick, maybe even die if they eat the buds. They will throw up, have belly aches, trouble breathing and may even pass out and die. Just handling the flowers without eating any of them can cause sensitive people to break out in rash."

His quiet voice and lowered eyes seemed to ring bells in my head. This was more of the lore that Mrs. Talbot had been telling me out in her woods.

"But those blue flowers are all over town! We have a big vase of them in the front of the church every Sunday morning in the summer. And I've read that the Queen Anne's Lace is a kind of a wild carrot."

Now the druggist smiled, again gently, but I seemed to see a glimmer of something less than benign in the pale blue eyes behind the thick glasses. "Well, I haven't been to your church, but you should remember that many blue flowers, not all, mind you, but many; are poisonous. Stocks and foxgloves are deadly; but, on the other hand, your bright blue bachelor buttons aren't. They even use them in salads in the Alps. And, it is true that Queen Anne's Lace is a type of carrot, and the root can be eaten, if properly prepared. But, what she has in this bouquet is deadly hemlock. That is the poison they used to kill Socrates, that old time Greek. Hemlock is also beautiful; and it is hard to tell the difference between it and the Queen Anne's Lace which is harmless, but hemlock is totally deadly."

Now, Judy seemed to come out of her cherry ice cream/dating fantasy cloud, enough to join the conversation.

"But she just picks these for my mother. Mother just loves the pretty green herby looking lacy flowers with the blues. She has me bring them to her with the leaves left on, so she can trim them to fit her vases. Makes a big mess of leaves in the kitchen sink, which she usually doesn't like, but she seems to like blue flowers so much she doesn't care."

"Well, you tell her to be careful handling them. And, you girls should be careful, too. We wouldn't want folks to think you were some kind of witchy women if they knew how dangerous these things are!"

"You know, in my youth, I lived in Europe." He paused, carefully not looking at us. Perhaps he felt he had talked too much, even to a few teenaged girls. "Even in those days, hundreds of years after we were supposedly enlightened, people in the villages away from the cities still believed in witches, some what. If a baby was born without a father, or a calf died, folks liked to crouch in their kitchens at night and whisper about who the witches were that were making the bad things happen. If you looked hard enough, there was always some old person around who was crazy, or talked to themselves, or brewed herbs. Or even were so poor they had to harvest mushrooms and berries to stay alive. And, when the people of the town figured out who the witch was, that person had to die. Of course, some silly types tried to be witches, to pretend to be powerful, but that is just sort of silly stuff. Swearing allegiance to the devil and all that sort of thing hardly ever works, I think. Witchcraft seems to me, to depend on making your customers believe in you. Any magic you are selling is really only right between their eyes." He paused again, and let out sort of a giggle;

then, seeming to forget his audience, continued, "Sort of like sex. Make them think you are great, or sexy, whatever, and you are."

He looked at us now, and seemed to mentally shake himself. "Well, you understand, there are lots of herbs that can cause folks to think and act silly or even hurt them. So you should always be careful, young women; don't let the town think you know more than they are comfortable with."

Chapter 21

A QUIET GIRL WHO NEVER MAKES TROUBLE

After leaving the dim drugstore that had seemed to change to a place of vague mystery, just while we were savoring our cherry vanilla ice cream cones, we were almost dazzled by the sunshine on the late afternoon town streets. I felt a little awed by Mr. Huffman's speech, and very, very curious about what he had said. Was he talking for my benefit? Did he sense that I sometimes understood more than the surface things about people? Was he trying to warn me of something or maybe hint of things I should be finding out?

"Well, that is just one weird old man!" As usual, Judy's thoughts seemed to just pop up in her head and flow immediately out her mouth. Sometimes I wondered if she was really as silly as she seemed, or if that was just an act.

"Oh, I don't know. He seems to like us. Probably just has stuff that has happened to him that he thinks about a lot." I wasn't sure if Judy had heard the gossip about the poor dead baby in the suitcase, but didn't feel like telling her about that, if not.

As usual, Suzie didn't look at us, but now she did pipe up from behind us, "I like him."

I always wondered about Suzie. She seemed pretty smart in a lot of ways, but she didn't talk much, just sort of followed in the wake left as Judy plowed her flamboyant way through the world. She struck me as being terribly aware of what was going on among the people around her, but she never seemed to raise her eyes to look at our faces. I think the teachers liked her in school because she never made any trouble in class. Just sat in the back of the room, was quiet and turned in grade B answers to all her tests. Not much trouble and she spent a lot of time in the library reading all sorts of stuff.

By the time we reached the girl's house on the other side of town, the shadows were getting longer, reaching into the late evening purple, and a few of the neighbors seemed to be getting home from school and work. Their house was set in the same standard pristine lawn, fluffy flowers, sparkling window venue, as the rest of the town; but when we walked up the steps, across the wooden porch and into the living room, the Norman Rockwell American world of the Saturday Evening Post outside seemed to slip far away.

While the room across from the living room, where Judy's mother gave piano lessons, was sparkling and shiny, with a huge bouquet of blue flowers spilling a blue-colored glow across the polished piano, the living room behind the half open door across from that studio was a study in disarray and neglect.

Judy's father, whom I had come to think of as a bad man, was sitting in a plastic covered chair, scowling at the small, round-screened, black and white television in the big shiny console. Although it was late in the afternoon, he lounged in wrinkled pajama bottoms and a dirty white tee shirt. His hair looked greasy and uncombed, and his matted beard that I had always remembered as being trimmed and dapper, sort of faded into the stray whiskers on the rest of his unshaven face. There was a definite unwashed smell about him, mingled with the smell of stale cigarettes. An overflowing ashtray sat in the middle of a scatter of ashes on the dusty table surface next to his chair. A half finished bowl of what looked like cold greasy chicken soup also sat on the end table next to the ash pile. Nestled in at the base of the table, almost, but not quite, out of sight, were a few empty beer bottles, their fumes adding to the pungent atmosphere of his retreat.

"You girls going out again tonight? Your mother is going to be gone. I'll need someone to stay home and take care of me tonight."

"Mary and I are going to the FFA, you know, the Future Farmers of America, square dance tonight. Her dad will pick her up there afterwards, but Suzie is too young to go, and she can stay with you.

Suzie, shoulders slumped more than usual, silently left the room, without making eye contact.

Chapter 22

THOSE BLUE FLOWERS THAT MOTHER LIKES

"Com'on, Mary, we have a little free time before we have to go over to the gym, lets go sit on the swing." Judy grabbed my arm firmly and hustled me out to the front porch to the white washed wooden swing.

"My dad is such a grouch! He has been sick a lot lately, with stomach aches and stuff, even with my mom making him nice chicken and rice soup to try to make him feel better. And he is always thirsty! 'Course, I don't think all that beer is really good for him. He keeps saying it cuts his thirst best, but I think he is just getting to be a sloppy old drunk. I learned a long time ago that when he had been drinking a lot he wouldn't be as mean to my mom and Suzie and me."

She stopped pushing the swing back and forth, and looked away from me, then said much quieter "But you don't need to know about all that family stuff. My mom is really good to him. She makes really good chicken soup for him all the time. We don't even eat it, but he likes it, and she puts lots of finely chopped parsley and other herbs in it, to make it really tasty for him. She isn't doing a lot of piano lessons now. Just that man from outside town, you know, he was getting a divorce, then his wife killed herself. So, I guess taking music lessons from my mom helps him forget all that bad stuff that has been happening to him lately. Betty and Brenda, you know, my friends from school, are his daughters and they say he is much happier since he has started taking lessons from my mom. And, I think helping him has been good for my mom, too, even with my dad being so sick and grouchy. She spends a lot of time with her student , arranging music for special events and even going over to his house after supper to work on arrangements and plans for upcoming programs. They like to work on their music without the girls around, so Betty and Brenda get to come into town those evenings and I get to go out riding around with them in their car. 'Course, that leaves Suzie here to take care of Dad, but she is young, and I don't think he is well enough to be too mean to her. I want to get you to know Betty and Brenda soon. You will have a lot in common with us all, I think. Suzie even likes them, and you know she doesn't really have any friends of her own."

Judy pursed her lips for a moment, then sighed and resumed her monologue, lowering her voice. "But that is enough about me! Let's talk about you. Are you going with me and the guys to the Marine Corp Ball? I really want you to come, and we will keep it real quiet. No need letting these noisy old biddies in this town know about it. We could have so much fun, and the guys will be real nice to us. And, maybe if they like us, they will invite us back or something! And we could still have a boyfriend in town here if one came along. Those marines wouldn't be able to come up to visit often, and no one would know anything about them. But, I bet if they did start coming up in the future they would really show us a good time. So, what do you think?"

Somehow, I had to think of a quick answer that wouldn't be too much of a promise of something that I had no intention of doing, and still keep me in her good graces.

"I'm not sure I could handle two boyfriends at the same time. Haven't even found one yet, but it sure is something to think about."

Then, hoping to get her off the point, "What is that red stuff all over your hands? It really looks gross. Do you think you want to go to the dance tonight with your hands looking like that?" It was sort of a mean trick, because I knew how important it was to Judy to look wonderful, but it got her off on a different path real fast.

"Oh, this! Well, you know you are right, my hands look like an old farm woman's, but I'll cover them with powder before we go, to hide the red. It is some sort of a rash, I get from picking those old blue flowers Momma like so much. She always says "Honey, be sure and get some of those with the leaves still around them; it sure makes them look pretty that way in the vase." So I do, then I break out something terrible. Guess I'm allergic or something. Old Mr. Huffmann is a crazy old coot, but maybe some of those flowers are a little rough on the skin, like he said.

"But I won't let a little thing like red hands keep me from going to a social occasion like a barn dance!"

Chapter 23

BARN DANCE, WHEN THE ANIMALS GET FRISKY AND THE OLD BULL WATCHES

The barn dance was pretty much like I thought it would be. The boys had piled the bales of hay in such a way that we had to crawl through tunnels in the dark to get into the gym. And, pretty predictably, half way through the tunnel, a hand reached out in the dark to try to locate a butt to pat, or at least snap a bra strap in the dark. I gave the expected obligatory squeal, then, setting my foot firmly down where I thought the other hand would be on the floor, pushed my way away from the whispering, complaining male voice in the dark. Somehow, getting pawed in the middle of a hay tunnel held little fear, or even secret delight for me, after some of my adventures last semester. I did sort of hope that it wasn't Jr. Jackson that had got a nice firm grip on my parts that were not meant to be grabbed. That would make it a little sleazier than it was, but of course, if it was Jr. I could feel a little better about stomping that poor hand in the dark.

The shop teacher that was in charge of the boys and their decoration of the gym probably knew of the secret pawing station in the tunnel, but he seemed to just keep a bland, smug face behind his thick glasses. Girls were meant for guys to sneak a feel from and the shop teacher probably thought of this as an educational experience for both the frustrated young males as well as those stuck-up girls. I wondered if he hadn't gotten enough of pawing girls when he was young and was just making up for any shortages of that now, listening to the indignant complaints of the girls and the male bonding snorts of the boys.

My dad was waiting in the truck in the parking lot at exactly 8:30. The dance was not particularly over, but as far as my father's timing went, it was. I am not sure if he thought that was the magic time that would make sure teenagers didn't get into trouble, or if that time would mean he could still get home to bed and to sleep at nine or so. I had learned that any time he had to pick me up from a school activity, 8:30 was the pick-up time that kept him from getting too grouchy.

Chapter 24

AFTER THE BALL

Later, back in the grey wooden house out in the fields, I tried to review my night and what, if anything, I had learned to report to the sheriff. First, and probably least important, was that the shop teacher over at the school was letting the boys set traps in the straw for a little fondling on passing females. Was the shop teacher condoning this, and was he maybe getting secret thrills out of the boys behaving as male animals? In other words, was he really a dirty old man as well as a teacher?

And, then, Judy's mother was giving lessons to Betty and Brenda's father out at his house at nights. He had just become a widower when his estranged wife, Betty and Brenda's mother, and Mrs. Talbot's daughter; had supposedly drawn her body up into a tight ball and shot herself with an ancient family shotgun.

Judy's mother was pretty happy these days, though her husband was still a rather nasty tempered old drunk, and sick on top of that. She had never in the past, struck me as being particularly happy, but it seemed that with this new student and her husband sick enough not to be so mean to her and the girls, her life was better. She was gone lots of nights, too; so Judy and Betty and Brenda got to go out in one of the smaller trucks and "drive around". I had to wonder what there was for them to see and do out there on the country roads late at night, but even though things were going pretty well for their mother, this didn't seem like a good reason for her to kill her student's wife.

For some reason, I was very uncom-fortable with the knowledge that little Suzie was left as the caregiver for her father these nights when everyone else was out. Somehow, her drooped shoulders and sad eyes that never quite met with other peoples', bothered me a great deal. And, Judy always seemed to be almost holding something back from me as well. Did all her silly teenage babble cover some darkness that I needed to know? I was not sure how I was going to report these uncomfortable feelings to the sheriff.

Mr. Huffman, the druggist, was a nice quiet man who seemed to have questions that he didn't ask, about the girls and their mother. Did he have ideas about what it was that the girls seemed to be trying to hide?

While these thoughts fluffed around like clouds in my brain, still in the background of my mind lingered the soft, perfumed smell of the blue flowers on Judy's mother's shiny, polished piano.

Chapter 25

MRS. TALBOT
WANTS TO TALK

Even though I hadn't quite organized my thoughts enough to give my report to the sheriff, the next morning at school, I had barely put my book in my desk and cracked open a note book when the office runner showed up, with a note that I had a guest downstairs.

The secretary in the office was getting tired of me popping in there in the middle of the school day at all hours, and merely waved me out to the front steps of the school. As I expected, the official sheriff's car was sitting at the curb, engine chugging, with the tailpipe merrily puffing out dark exhaust.

"You're real early this morning, aren't you."

"Yeah." The sheriff rubbed his jaw with the hand in which he was clutching the half smoked cigarette. "I just got to work and got coffee, then, there was a letter from your friend, Mrs. Talbot. She mailed it a couple of days ago, and marked it 'Important', so I guess we should get out there pretty soon. Funny thing is, she particularly wanted me to bring you. Said she really needed to talk to you. Didn't seem that eager to talk to me; guess I got invited to this party to be your chauffeur, if nothing more."

Mrs. Talbot's house seemed strangely quiet when we drove up, and looking at the empty porch and closed door, it took me a minute to figure out that the dogs weren't there to greet us.

Then, Mrs. Talbot came to the door and called down to us. "''Bout time you got here, Pete Olsen. I want to talk to Mary alone for a little bit, then I'll see about you."

So, leaving a scowling sheriff in the car, I climbed the steps of the cabin and went in.

The first thing I noticed was a scarred, cardboard suitcase sitting by the door.

"Are you going somewhere? Where are the dogs?"

Mrs. Talbot busied herself, pouring two cups of coffee from the blue enamel pot, then, set the pot in the sink before she turned to me. "I left the dogs at the neighbors. I hope my granddaughters take them, but didn't have time to talk to them, without a phone."

She set the cups on the little table opposite of me, and then continued. "And, it looks like I will be riding into town with you and the sheriff in a little while, so thought I might as well get ready.

"Mary, things are just so strange in

this life. I always thought I would have a house full of children and grandchildren all my life. My husband and I worked hard to make a life for us and to have something to leave them, but now they don't need me, and this home I have struggled to build and grow will just become something they will sell for whatever they can get out of it when I die. And, it would be convenient for them if that was pretty soon.

"I made the big mistake of loaning them money a few years ago, more money than I could afford; when they were having trouble with the business. I didn't mind doing it. I thought that would make us all closer. But it didn't. They just stopped coming to see me altogether. Think maybe they were embarrassed, then, decided that I was a mean old woman when I asked for some of it back. Somehow, honey, 'loans' to relatives just don't get repaid, and the person that does the lending becomes the bad guy in the long run.

"Funny thing is, I don't mind losing the money as much as I mind losing them. Sometimes I get mad, and wonder how I could have raised kids that didn't care any more than that for me, but usually, I just feel sad.

"So, Mary, it has been good for me to have you interested in me, and I wanted you to have this to remember me by." Now, she laid a small, sort of shabby box on the table in front of me. When I opened it, a beautiful long necklace of round green rock beads glowed on the shabby old velvet lining the old box. "I bought this on my honeymoon, in Hong Kong. My husband and I went there to be missionaries to the Chinese, many, many years ago, but, the revolution started in China and we had to come back home.

"There is another large box of the jewelry I gathered over the years to bequeath to my beloved descendants. I guess now it will just go to which ever bidder makes the best bid at the auction to unload my junk. No one will know or care about this beautiful jade necklace I bought in Hong Kong on my honeymoon and have saved for years to give to my treasured granddaughters, or even the handsome young man I was with at the time, that later became their grandfather. So, I wanted to give this to you, so there will be some memory of my husband and me. Strange, he has been dead almost fifty years now, and I will be joining him soon, I guess, but I can still remember the day he bought that necklace for me in Kowloon. We were waiting next to the ferryboat landing to catch a sampan to ride to the little outer island where our parish was going to be.

"Now, I suppose, when I die, relatives will come out of the woodwork, and descend like vultures to divvy up the spoils without ever caring about the history of my old treasures, or me.

"So, Mary, I want you to know that I still love my granddaughters, and would do anything I could for them, even after all these years. Their mother got caught-up with watching those crazy TV shows on a Sunday afternoon, and decided she should have them dressing in long dresses and give half the family money to that crazy evangelist that is always asking for folks to send their money in to promote his healing. Just real crazy stuff, but she had decided she could buy her way into heaven and turn the girls into saints or something. So, it wasn't their fault that they weren't really taught to care about me, when their momma was trying to take all their money and fun away. But, I hope after I am gone, that they will think kindly of me. And, I want you to have my necklace just because you will understand that I have done a lot of foolish things out of love, but at least I did love. I guess a lot of folks don't even have that comfort when they get to the end of their life.

"Now, if you could call the sheriff in, I guess it is time I talked to him."

Chapter 26

REVEREND GLENDA OFFERS SHELTER

On the ride back to town, we were almost totally silent. Mrs. Talbot sat in the back seat with her suitcase on the floor by her feet looking out the window at the countryside going by. She seemed to be saying good bye to her trees and life among them forever. The sheriff, his jaw tight and twitching, was driving, frowning at the road a lot more than usual. I sat with my hand in the pocket of my jacket, running my fingers over the smooth jade beads of the necklace Mrs. Talbot had given me, as I thought.

Something was wrong! Dreadfully, dreadfully wrong! When the sheriff went into the cabin, I had gone out to the front porch to pretend not to listen to their con- versation, but in the mountain stillness I had heard Mrs. Talbot tell the sheriff in a voice not much louder than a whisper that she had shot her daughter. She was lying! I knew that, but things were too confused in my head to sort out why I knew she was ly- ing, or even why she was confessing to murder.

When we got back to the sheriff's of- fice, the sheriff, still scowling at the world, sat Mrs. Talbot in his waiting room with her suitcase by her feet. I slipped into the wooden chair by her and reached over to hold her bony hand. We sat without speak- ing and could see the sheriff, still scowling through the glass door of the office, frown- ing and talking on the black phone on his desk. He almost slammed the phone down on his first conversation, then immediately picked the phone up and dialed it again. He hunched over the phone, and talked again, this time with more animation, almost smiling into the plastic mouth piece. Finally, he hung up, and came out to where we were.

"Okay, now here's what we're going to do," He said to us. "I talked to Judge Phillips and he agreed with me that this jail is no place for Mrs. Talbot to be sitting while we figure stuff out. So, called Reverend Glenda, and she says Mrs. Talbot should come over to her house and stay." He turned to Mrs. Talbot, "Believe me, Ma'am you wouldn't want to be spending much time in that cell, where all the Saturday night warriors have slept off twenty years worth of drunk.

"Mary, I'll drop you off at the school after we get Mrs. Talbot settled and comfortable."

The Reverend Glenda was as usual, a warm little woman who immediately greeted Mrs. Talbot with a long hug, and a cup of coffee. By now, the old mountain lady seemed to have visibly aged before our eyes, despite her earlier resolve, and almost collapsed into a soft armchair seemingly overcome by the compassion and the coffee.

Chapter 27

GETTING TO KNOW THE GIRLS

The sheriff spoke a minute with Reverend Glenda who had already assumed a protective, hovering presence around Mrs. Talbot. Then, I kissed her leathery cheek and whispered my good-bye, and the sheriff whisked me away to try to catch up with my History of Missouri class at my high school jail, only slightly better, I thought, than the cell he had refused to put Mrs. Talbot in. I seemed to be missing a lot of that Missouri History, Lewis and Clark adventure, these days; but supposed I could catch up with those guys later when my own adventures were a little less time consuming.

As usual, when I came into class late

from doing work with the sheriff, heads turned, and silent questioning eyes followed me to the front desk, where I handed my pass to the teacher. She hardly glanced at it, but frowned at me and waved me to my seat without speaking.

After class, as I was pressing out into the hall, I felt a sharp pinch on my arm, and Judy, from behind me, breathed into my ear. "Look, I want you to come to the restroom after school. My sister and I, and the girls, get together after school every day, and we have something we want to talk to you about."

The "girls" Judy was talking about completed the little bevy of teens that the sheriff had wanted me to question, so I was willing to let my self be forced into joining a meeting with them. I thought about letting it slip that I had been with the sheriff when he picked up their grandmother for shooting their mother, but then decided to keep quiet; they would find out about that soon enough.

So, I plastered on a rather innocent smile and listened as Judy explained their purpose in meeting me. "We have a little, well, a sort of a study group that meets at night when my mom goes out to their dad's house to give piano lessons to their dad. We even drove out and talked to their grandma about stuff that grows in the woods, a while back. And, we are studying herbs and crystals and things, and are learning how to dance in the moonlight and make things happen. We have instruction, of course, but the way it works is that we have to do the spells and stuff by ourselves."

"Wow! Who is teaching you all this stuff? It sounds awfully complicated." Still, the same vanilla smile.

"Oh, we can't talk about that, it has to stay a 'secret social group'. But, here is the thing, if you join, that would be five of us, and five is a really good number for our group. We would be a real pentagon then..."

[*Pentagram-they mean pentagram!*].

I was growing pretty apprehensive about this meeting and thought I should get out as soon as possible. Hopefully this would be something positive to report to the sheriff.

"And we know you know things. Like you read a lot of stuff, and live out there on that farm with all those plants around and we could show you how to use them. We know you would like to get that father of yours off your back, hmm? And we know how to help you! Mary, you are almost out of high school, and you need to be able to go where you want when you want, and he is just unreasonable!"

I shifted my weight, trying to keep all of them in sight, now. Somehow, without any really obvious move, they had re-grouped and seemed intent on gathering around me from all sides.

They looked at each other, then moved closer to me and their eyes were not really so blank now, but throbbing and sinister. I saw the girls were now into another place. I sensed rather than saw, a fiery blue green glow in the room, then, I saw the two girls in my line of sight suddenly start to grin at the girl that was directly behind me. I twirled my head to the side enough to see that girl making a sign of the cross, but upside down, using her big rhinestone handled fingernail file and grinning at the other girls. I elbowed my way through the four sided block and pushed my back almost against the painted cement wall where I could watch all four at once. I didn't think this was going to work out so well. *Try to be cool. Wouldn't do to show fear.*

"I don't join things much, you know, living out in the country, I can't really go to meetings at night and that sort of stuff." Lame grin.

"But, Mary, you would like what we do." The other girls were now grinning as well, and maybe on an individual level, it might have just been a sort of silly grin, but now, on the faces of the combined watchers, I felt a sense of skin prickling danger, like watching a snake you know is too deadly, and too, too close.

Chapter 28

DARK LADY

Suddenly, the door banged open, and the doorway was filled by a tall, dark, adult figure, that only paused for a moment, silhouetted in the fading afternoon sunlight from the far off door at the end of the long hall. Then, with a surging whirl, the dark force swept in and seemed to engulf us and the whole dingy bathroom with her presence.

"O there you are! Honey, I have been looking all over this dumpy, little school for you!"

"Angelique!?" Amazingly, for once I was almost speechless.

"Girls," the husky contralto voice came almost as a loud purr as Angelique glanced at the group of the suddenly deflated teenaged girl gang, staring at this strange, exotic black woman who had blown in from nowhere like a gust of wind clamoring into their midst "Has somebody got a cigarette for me, I am just dying!"

The girls continued to stare in amazement. Then one of them pulled a shiny "Glamour Lady" pack from her pocket and shook out a cigarette that she silently extended at arms length for Angelique. Judy popped open a pink rhinestone lighter, and still at arm's length, shot a flickering flame to light Angelique's smoke. Angelique took a deep inhale, grimaced, then, laughed. "O, my goodness girl! That is one miserable drag. You children should at least learn to go with the grown-up smokes if you are going to try to dabble. Com'on Mary, lets blow this joint."

She grabbed my arm and hustled me out the door and down the hall, leaving the four girls still wide mouthed and drooping behind.

"Now what was that all about?" The honeyed accent she had used in the bathroom had slipped from her voice now. Somehow, she sounded almost mannish, I thought, and a little peeved.

"I don't know, they wanted me to join some sort of secret society or something. Just kid stuff, you know."

The black woman snorted, "Just "kid's stuff"! Mary, honey, those girls just don't know how deep that water they are trying to wade in is."

"Angelique, I can't believe it is you! What are you doing here, anyway. We don't even have any black people in this town!"

"Honey, I know how to read a road map, and I decided to visit you in this silly little burg, Jim Crow be damned! Actually, some nice truck driver knew where to drop me, and then finding the school wasn't that hard. I've seen these pokey little southern towns before, five churches, two taverns, and a big honky high school. All lily white! Now, how hard is that to figure out?"

Then I had to put a hug around my friend's strong shoulders. "I'm real glad to see you, anyway. But I thought you were staying down in Cuba with Jimmy for awhile."

"Our job in Cuba got a little too hot when your friend, El Caballo, came into power. He is a nice man, definitely a stud, and all that; but he is for sure hanging with the Russians. And he's out in the open about admitting it now! So things were starting to really heat up in Havana, and the boss in DC pulled us out. WhiteStar had already left; think maybe she has more or less retired. Now they sent Jimmy on a new assignment, and I was sort of waiting to get reassigned, too. So, thought since I was going to be going up north, anyway, I would see if I could look you up and see what is going on with you." We paused on the broad steps of the school. Angelique looked around at the other students waiting to get on the buses and craning their necks to see what I was doing with a tall black woman. "Now, Mary, I know your family would be shocked if I showed up at your house, and I doubt if there is a cheap motel around that would take a single black gal, so do you have any ideas where I could stay for a few days? Guess I could hide out in your Dad's barn, but that isn't quite where a lady should have to stay."

I had to think about that. I was ashamed to admit to this kind and under-standing friend that my family, and in fact most of the folks of the town I lived in, would be put off by her rich warm skin tones. My dad had, over several years time, come to more or less accept our neighbor, Mr. Leroy, who came wrapped in a plain brown wrapper. Dad wouldn't admit to lik-ing his neighbor, but he seemed to have made a grudging acceptance of the fact that our neighbors were Negroes and they hadn't killed us in our beds. Fortunately, I thought, for the whole equation, was the fact that on the other side of the racial fence, Mr. Leroy was just as prejudiced against our paleness as Dad was against his dark skin. Somehow, the two men seemed to function somewhere on the middle of the seesaw by holding a working balance between mutually held racism and neighborly respect.

"Let me take you over to my Grandma' Elkins house. Grandpa just died a few weeks ago, and she is pretty lonely there by herself. She wouldn't mention you to my dad, and she wouldn't mind that you are a black woman. My bus doesn't run for about an hour, so, I can take you over to her house, and still be back in time to catch it, so my folks won't even know."

Chapter 29

Tennie Has a Guest

When we got to my Indian grandma's house, she gave one rather sharp look at Angelique, then sat us down on the couch and bustled around getting us glasses of ice tea.

"Grandma, this is my friend, Angelique. I met her when Uncle Perry and I went on that trip down south. Angelique, this is my Grandma Elkins. Grandma, I need a big favor. Angelique will be here for a few days, and needs a place to stay. There wouldn't be room out on the farm, besides, you know how my dad is. Would it be okay if she stayed here with you? Just for a few days and that way I can still come over and visit, and maybe you would like company, too?" Almost finished with a whine on that, but I figured Grandma knew how my dad was, anyway.

"Sure, honey. And you're right, it would be sorta nice to have someone around to talk to. Angelique, we'll have to straighten up that back bedroom a little and maybe get some of the dust out of there. I've got clean sheets washed, so we'll change those. Hasn't even been anybody in that room in a couple of months, but we should be able to fix it up okay." Grandma was smiling and chatting with Angelique; almost bustling, as she figured out how to make her unexpected guest comfortable, and she seemed to barely notice when I said good bye to them and left to catch the last school bus out to the ditch dump road and home.

Chapter 30

ANGELIQUE LETS HER HAIR DOWN TO TENNIE

After Mary had left, the two women worked with only a little chatter, cleaning up the spare room, and pulling a supper of heated up chicken soup and biscuits from Tennie's fridge. Then, as the evening turned purple, they settled on the wide old porch with glasses of Tennie's "special health juice drink" that she had made with fermented grapes from Mary's farm.

Stretching her legs to a comfortable position, Tennie finally raised the question that the other woman had been more or less expecting.

"Angelique, how is it that you have fooled Mary all this time?"

The silence stretched on, seemingly forever, then, Angelique laughed, "Damned if I know, Miss Tennie! Think the idea of a man becoming a woman is just something that she has never considered. Now, she thinks I am a really strong woman, but she hasn't really noticed the beard stubble too much, and I wear a scarf over the Adam's apple, so she just thinks that it is just sort of a fashion thing. She also accepts that I am different, and doesn't pay as much attention, as a lot of older people would. Maybe that is because I come wrapped in a brown skin. She is a good kid, and I think it doesn't freak her out that her best friend is a black woman with a deep voice. I'm sure that is unlike most of the folks around here."

"What about your friend, the Korean? Mary told me a little about him."

"Jimmy? I know what you are thinking, but Jimmy is an all 100 percent good ol' all American, well, all American/Korean-boy. He is straight as they come. I think it is because he is so really macho that he can be okay with the idea that his lady love used to use the men's rooms in the bars. He is out of country now; something he is doing for the government. He can't, well, he won't, tell me much; but I suspect that it has something to do with the problems that are building up in Asia again. They are saying that we will never get into another war, not after WWII. But he was in that 'police action' in Korea, undercover intelligence stuff, of course, and he claimed it was as bad a 'war' as you would ever want to see.

"Now they are trying to rebuild the south part of Korea, but it was so devastated by the war that it is hard. The Japanese occupied that country from about 1900 until the end of WWII and they took all the natural resources back to Japan; all the trees went down, and the metals were taken to Japan to build up their war machines. They were tough and mean to the Koreans, and this raping that country's resources went on for forty-five years or so. Then, when the Japanese were finally defeated at the end of WWII, the 'Conflict' started. Those hills have been bombed until they are bare. No firewood, anywhere. Korea is a really cold country, and Jimmy told me that right after the war, the Americans were in there trying to rebuild the roads; but at night, the local folk would sneak out and take up the asphalt the Americans had laid in the daytime, to burn to keep warm. Must have smoked and smelled like crazy; but when your family is freezing, I guess you do anything to keep them alive."

"Well, I guess he would be a good spy, looking like all those other Koreans, but it's a shame we can't stop all this craziness over there."

"Oh, Ms. Tennie, he's not in Korea

now. I am pretty sure that he is in that peninsula with Indo-China on it. 'Vietnam', they call themselves. Nobody knows much about it in the states, but the communists are trying to take over that country, too.

"Then, there is trouble brewing in Thailand, and Burma and on the island that we used to call Formosa; that just changed their name to Taiwan, which used to be a part of mainland China. Now the Red Chinese want it back! All sorts of things boiling up, and they are all sort of connected. So if one country goes communist, the rest will just sort of follow along; what they call a domino effect. The old guy in the white house is worried about all this stuff. Probably seems like they are coming at him from all sides. He has called folks like Jimmy and your brother in because he is really beset with more problems than he can get a handle on; and those problems look to get worse before they go away."

"My brother? Oh, Perry's retired now, and I am sure he isn't going back into all that mess."

Angelique gave a very unladylike snort. "I know Perry thinks he is retired, but the President is an old friend, and I'm betting he is going to call all his markers in on this one."

Quieter, then, wistfully, she said, "Wouldn't mind retiring, myself. But I am known for having some special skills that they always seem to need on occasion, and I am on my way to be reassigned. Think they are going to send me out there with that Bob Hope Christmas tour. They even have that 'blonde bombshell', Jayne Mansfield, set to go with them to entertain the troops on Guam, Japan and some other places. Probably have me listed with the crew as a wardrobe mistress or something, then I will just sort of vanish on Guam and take care of whatever it is that I have to do.

'Course, you won't mention me or this to anyone. Not even real sure who I will be dealing with; just that it is undercover work, and it is important.

"Anyway, just thought since I was moving cross the country kind of on the quiet, I would stop here and visit Mary. She is a special sort of kid, and gives me a lot of hope for what is going to happen in our future. Sometimes my jobs are just so crazy I need to remember I have friends like Mary. I just don't know why I didn't realize that this 'heartland' was smack in the middle of the good-old-boys-with-the-white-sheets neighborhood, or I might have been better prepared."

Angelique smiled now, seeming to change the subject. "Now, listen, I sure do appreciate you putting me up. Just don't want to get you in any trouble. So, think I might just catch the bus or train out tomorrow so things won't have time to get nasty here for you and the rest of Mary's family."

Tennie gave a snort of derisive laughter. "Oh, they wouldn't bother me. I'm old, and known to have a mean temper. Those boys that would try to give you trouble sort of back down when it comes to someone who is not afraid. But you aren't going to be able to catch a bus or train out until the Saturday night bus, at the earliest, and I wouldn't advise you to start walking out of town. Too much open land out there, where a person like yourself could just vanish into one of the drainage ditches."

Chapter 31

CINNAMON ROLL JAIL

The next morning, I really wanted to sneak out of school and get over to Grandma Elkins to visit with Angelique, but felt like I had to check in with the sheriff and find out what was happening with Mrs. Talbot's case first. I hadn't told my parents about Mrs. Talbot, or about the girls wanting me to be a part of their "social club" or certainly not about Angelique being in town. So I finished my breakfast, cleaned up the kitchen and took my books and my younger sister to catch the bus out on the gravel road like any other day, waving at them as we passed the barn.

When we got to town, though, I had Mr. Emerson, our one-eyed school bus driver drop me off before school, close to the city hall, where the jail and the sheriff's office was.

The sheriff was frowning into his phone when I walked into his little office. He nodded at me when I came in then continued to talk quietly into his phone for a few minutes, finally hanging up with almost a bang.

"Damned! Harland is getting antsy about me having Mrs. Talbot over at the Reverend Glenda's. I told him that I think she's lying. Just don't think that an 87 year old woman would shoot her own daughter. But, no! And I know he wants to follow the damned law to the letter, and I know he doesn't believe that either! Wants to charge her, get her set up for a court date, and stick her in a trial. Might as well just take her out and shoot her now!

"And I told him about the bawling out she gave me when I booked her. She said that the business had been in that family for five generations and, her granddaughters deserve to have a good life and a start for their future. Said she was ashamed of her daughter wanting to divide it up and destroy everything. Imagine, pulling it out from under your own children like that! Mrs. Talbot said I should tell Harland, whom she has known all his life, that he should realize that she would do anything she had to do to protect her family. She said she had killed twenty-eight poisonous snakes out there in the country over the years, and this was just another threat to her family that she had to get rid of.

"Now, Mary, I may not be as smart as you at reading folks, but she was crying all the time she told me all that, and I just don't believe her!"

Thinking of my impressions of Mrs. Talbot, and her granddaughters, I tended to agree with him, but still had some things to work out of this ball of yarn. The girls weren't little kids that needed protecting. And, they certainly weren't so close that they would be going out to talk to her about things that grew in the woods a lot. I could understand the old woman wanting to protect them if they were little kids, but as almost adults, it just didn't seem that they were as helpless as she thought.

"I think you are right to keep her over at the Reverend Glenda's house. She is an old lady, and the Reverend will take good care of her. I know she doesn't like being in town, but at least she is with someone who cares about her."

The sheriff grinned at that. "Yeah, I talked to Glenda real early this morning, and she was baking cinnamon rolls for Mrs. Talbot's breakfast. Bless her heart! Sounded so good, I almost thought maybe I should go over to check on my prisoner in a little while, and see if there are any of those rolls left over after breakfast."

Now, the cinnamon roll inspired grin dropped from his face. "So, did you talk to those girls like I asked you to?"

I had to stop and think before I answered. Didn't really want to tell him about Angelique being in town; too many explanations there about who she was and how I had got to know her that I didn't really want to get into.

And the girls he wanted me to talk to had given me almost as many feelings of apprehension as they had raised unanswered questions.

"I talked to them, and think there is something there I need to sniff out some more before I bring it to you. You have enough going on here without more things to think about."

Chapter 32

A TRIP TO THE GROCERY

After leaving the sheriff to ponder his problems with Mrs. Talbot and muse about those cinnamon rolls, I crossed town at a brisk walk, over the old brick sidewalks, stirring up the leaves that were starting to already settle down before the fall. By the time I reached the big high school, I had come to some conclusions about things, and felt I had to definitely get away from the school today so that I could think unhampered by all that nonsense in the classroom. Louis and Clark could just forge on without me for one more day. So, I went into the principal's office, trumped up an excuse of working on official business today, and ducked back on the street to walk over to Grandma Tennie's old house, across town.

My Indian grandma and Angelique were out pottering in Grandma's garden when I walked up the path. Angelique was holding a pan with tomatoes in it, and Grandma had moved from gathering tomatoes to snipping some of her favorite salad herbs. Parsley, basil and oregano were piling up in a bounty in Angelique's pan.

When I came into the yard, they bustled me back to the house, and we all relaxed with freshly brewed iced tea on the porch, while I gave them a slightly edited version of why I wasn't in school today.

After our tea, Angelique stood up and stretched. "Mary, since you are sort of out on a self granted parole from the school, how about we take a little walk around town. You know, like sightseeing. Always like to get the lay of the land in a place, and I need to pick up some things down town, anyway."

I think my grandma and I both considered this sort of a bad idea in this town, but I knew when Angelique got an idea she would follow through on it either with or without me. So, a little while later, she and I were strolling down the two block long main street of the town.

The bench on the corner of the intersection that was usually the watch point of the men my dad referred to as those "lazy town peckerheads" was empty when we went by, so that seemed fairly promising to me.

My optimism was dimmed, though, when we walked into the grocery store. The owner of the grocery, Mr. Jenkins, had always been a smiling kindly looking man. But today, his blue eyes were cold and steely when he looked at us.

"Mary, you can shop here, but your 'friend' will have to go around to the back."

I could feel the blood leave my face and started to speak when Angelique pulled me back and whispered, "Here, Mary. Here's $5. Pick up a pound of bacon, loaf of bread, dozen eggs, a can of that evaporated milk that your grandma likes in her coffee, a bottle of milk; oh, and get about a half dozen of those oranges that I smell." Then, she turned and quickly stepped out on the sidewalk, and vanished in the alley at the side of the store.

I was burning at this treatment of my friend, but got the groceries that she wanted. After Mr. Jenkins checked them through and bagged them, I laid the $5 bill down on the counter silently, and just as silently, he counted out the change and laid it on the counter. Then still not speaking, he picked up the $5 bill and looking at me with a scowl, dropped it into the trash basket next to the check out counter.

Looking at his cold face, I suddenly

flashed on what would happen next.

He'll wait until I'm gone, then get it out and put it in the drawer. He just wants to be hateful.

I left then, but could still feel the cold anger burning me when I stepped out on the sidewalk and Angelique came out of the alley to join me.

"Now, it's okay, Mary, I should have known what to expect. Should have just sent you down here in the first place, but I figured Mrs. Tennie could use a little time off from having to entertain company all day."

Our shadows were moving under us right at the eleven thirty point when we passed the corner gossip bench, and now the old men that liked to watch the town were out, slouching on it. They were scowling, and watching our progress down the street. None of them spoke when we walked by, but from the corner of my eye, I could see the heads turn to watch us pass, and feel their frowning eyes on our backs as we crossed the railroad tracks and walked down the little lane, to the old wooden house where my grandma lived.

 # Chapter 33

Nap Time

After a lunch of fresh tomatoes dusted with finely chopped basil, sliced onto the store-bought white bread that Angelique and I had bought and slathered with Miracle Whip, we again retreated to the cool shade of the front porch. Resting in the shade with the sleepy sound of the bees that were enjoying Grandma's hollyhocks, I told them most of the details of the investigation of the dead woman, and even the dead horses, that the sheriff and I were conducting.

Grandma sat quietly for a time after I finished talking about the girls and the poisonings and the poor dead lady, then spoke quietly. "I think you are closer than you think in finding an answer to these things. You are just sort of letting your worry cloud what you know. If you just relax and rest, your brain will have a chance to think about these things without all the distractions you are putting in front of it."

Angelique gave a soft chuckle then. "Sounds like your grandma thinks it is time you took a nap, young lady! Probably a good idea at that." So, on the advice of two of my favorite ladies, I turned off my motor and let the soft swinging of Grandma's faded hammock carry me away from the day.

And when I awoke, I knew what I had to tell the sheriff.

Chapter 34

A CHAT WITH THE SHERIFF

After leaving Grandma and Angelique, I headed back across the town, but instead of pushing on to the school, I turned into the sheriff's office again. Plopping myself down in front of his desk, I said, "Think it is time I told you about what the girls at the school are doing. And, I am going to need you to go over to talk to the coroner one more time.

"Then, I think I can tell you how all this happened. But I still think there is more to this than we know yet. And I sort of think you need to have a talk with Judy's mom, as well. I'm not sure if she is a part of the other stuff that I think is going on, but you need to find out."

The sheriff carefully set his feet flat on the floor behind his desk, and leaned forward on the paper littered surface of the desk to frown at me.

"Okay, young lady, what do you think is going on? And, what do you think Judy's mom has to do with that lady out there in the country getting shot?"

"Okay, this is sort of confusing. But, well, the girls are trying to do the old witchcraft stuff. I'm not sure where they have learned about it, and I don't think they know enough about it yet to do it well, but they are running around at night in Betty and Brenda's dad's truck while Judy's mom is out at his house giving him piano lessons."

The sheriff's eyebrows sort of shot up at that, and he thoughtfully placed a hand over his mouth, "Yeah, piano lessons."

"I am not sure, but I think Suzie is going on some of those rides with them, but she has to stay at home a lot and take care of her and Judy's father, so she may not know everything that they are doing. I know she and the girls went out to see Mrs. Talbot after the death of Mrs. Talbot's daughter, you know, Betty and Brenda's mother. Anyway, back to the witchcraft thing. Judy did sort of let slip that there was a leader to their group; they call them a 'coven' in the books, but I don't think the girls are really good enough to be real witches. I couldn't find out who their leader was, but I wonder if they are finding out stuff from Mrs. Talbot, who seems to know a lot of stuff about poisons in the plants, though I don't think she would want them to poison anyone, or do silly teenaged witch sort of stuff. But she might have told them some things without realizing they were planning on anything."

"Now wait a minute. You're talking poison, like what happened to the horses.

Mrs. Talbot has already admitted to shooting her daughter."

"Yeah, I think she did shoot her daughter." Now, I was getting excited and had the sheriff's undivided attention. "But, when we saw the body at the coroner's it was drawn into a ball, and Dr. Grace mentioned that there wasn't much blood. Now, when she took me out to investigate the dead horses with her, they were drawn like that body. She said that it was because they died from poisoning; that the bodies contorted that way. I think she was just so upset by the dead lady that she didn't see the connection in animal deaths and human deaths."

"But she had half her face shot away?"

"That is what made me think about this. When a dead body is shot, there isn't much blood left to leak out. The vet noticed that, but was already thinking she died from the gunshot, so, didn't really think about why there wasn't more blood. I think what happened then was that somehow Mrs. Talbot found out about the poisoning. Think probably the girls told her. Now, she loves those granddaughters, but she knows they are not smart enough to get away with it for long. When she found out the girls are dabbling, she was afraid the villagers would think they had poisoned their mother. So, she went over, got her son-in-law's gun, fired a shot into her dead daughter's face and jammed the gun between her knees. The legs were probably already drawn up so tight with that rigor mortis thing that that was the best she could do. Now, she is a smart old lady, but I don't think she ever had training in how to fake a suicide. Doesn't matter! Dr. Grace, she really hates that job you know, just did the quickest look at it she could and called it death by her own hand."

The sheriff's frown had steadily fumed while I had told him this. "So the teenaged girls really poisoned their mother to keep her from breaking up the family business and ruining their life. Sounds crazy, but maybe? What little monsters! And, they are young enough they won't get much more than a slap on the wrist!" He was now flushed a deep ruddy glow now, and I almost expected to see smoke coming from his ears. "Mrs. Talbot certainly didn't do them any favors by trying to cover for them. I would have thought she would have more sense than that."

"Maybe she shouldn't have done it, but you have to remember that she is a really old lady, and she loves those granddaughters and hadn't gotten to see them much in the past. She probably figured that she could live a few years in prison, and it wouldn't be too bad, because the girls would get to live a normal life. She is 87, and should never go to jail, anyway, but it would kill her just as fast to have her grand-daughters go to jail. Either way, they are minors. What will the judge do to them?"

The sheriff got up now, and poured a cup of cold greasy coffee for himself, glanced at me, then poured a second chipped ceramic mug, and clunked it down in front of me.

"I have no idea what Harland is going to do in this case. Even if the old lady didn't really do it, she covered up for the girls, and there has to be at least a half-dozen laws she is breaking. And you are right, she shouldn't go to jail." He took a sip of the cold cup, grimaced and ran a bony hand over his thin hair. "But you are wrong on one thing. She wouldn't last a year in a pris-on cell. Now, those girls, I don't know, maybe if they got into a good home situ-ation they would realize how crazy they were and get straightened out. But, I guarantee you, if they go into jail for a few years, they won't ever have a chance to go back to a 'real life', like she would like for them. Just too many folks in those prisons that are already too tainted for them to come out 'normal'. It is sort of a training school for hardened criminals. Thing is, Harland is such a tight son of a..., well, so 'up--tight' like you kids would say, that he will have to punish all of them someway. Sort of sorry for him, myself. Not sure how I would handle it either, if I was in his shoes."

"When are you going to talk to him?"

"Not for a few days. Probably good for the old lady to stay separate from folks. And, Harland likes to be in charge, so maybe he will be trying to think of what to do with her and realize he has to comprom- ise somewhere."

"Too bad he can't let her go back out to her cabin and have her granddaughters live there with her to take care of her. She'd like that, and the girls would probably learn a lot of good things from her."

The sheriff frowned at me. "Well, Miss Mary, you will have to learn someday, that things don't always work the way you would like to see them." He sounded really mad at that one. "Sometimes good people get hurt, and then I have to be the one to clean up their messes." The coffee cup set down hard enough to splash cold coffee on a stack of unopened mail.

Chapter 35

A MAGIC NICKEL

"Okay. I'm going over to talk to the girls right now. And you, Missy, are coming with me. You're going to listen to them and between you and me, maybe we'll figure something out."

"I don't know where they are at, maybe still at the school."

"Okay, we'll start there."

When we pulled up to the school in the official vehicle with the lights flashing, though, the school was dark and deserted, except for the handful of rural kids waiting around the parking lot for the second bus ride to get them home.

When I went over to talk with some of them, they told me that Betty and

Brenda had walked over to Judy's house with her after school.

So we drove quietly over there, then went in to find all the girls together in the house.

The four of them were clustered to-gether in a sort of invisible circle when we got there and rang the door bell. Somehow, their collective armor seemed to be up around them, and I think even the sheriff felt the wall between them and us.

Again, I noticed the huge bouquet of hydrangeas occupying the shiny piano top through the open door to the studio. Here in the small, almost dusty little den across the hall, another arrangement of blue stocks and lacy white hemlock blooms sat on a side table.

"Are your folks home? Not that an old guy like me doesn't like getting a chance to talk to four beautiful young women like yourselves." The sheriff was stretching himself hard to be the loveable clown with the girls, but their blank, stiff faces told me that no one was really buying his act.

"No, Mother is out, and Daddy is sleeping. He has been having a bad spell again, and needs his rest." Judy spoke for the group, seeming to be the silently selected leader for her sister and the other girls.

"Well," the sheriff slipped into the plan I knew he had all along, "I guess I could just talk to you girls for a few minutes, if that is okay."

Turning to Betty and Brenda, he continued on his general path that I knew was paved with good old country bull, "And, young ladies, I just wanted to say how sorry I am for the death of your mother."

The sisters quickly exchanged glances, then nodded and made polite little remarks, without really meeting his eyes.

"I know you have probably heard that we are holding your granny to answer some questions about this thing. Hope we can get clear on what happened soon."

Now, real clouds appeared on Brenda and Betty's faces, but before they could speak, Judy quickly spoke up. "Oh, their grandmother is a nice old lady, and they are worried about her, but know she will be okay. We all drove out to her cabin not long after their mother died, and she was just so glad to see us, and everything. We know you won't let them hurt her. But now it is probably time you left. All these questions are just too hard on the girls. They are going through a very hard time, you know; what with the mourning their mother and stuff."

Judy continued to stand between us and the pair of sisters, while her little sister, Suzie, had backed over close to the door. As usual, Suzie stood silent, with slumped shoulders and averted eyes.

"Well, Miss Judy, I guess you are right, and I am glad you are here, taking such good care of these girls in their hour of pain." The sheriff, I decided, knew when to back off even if it was just from a teenaged boss for the group.

As we were herded toward the door by the three older girls, he stopped in front of Suzie, and smiling, reached toward her face. "Honey, how can you hear the birds sing when you have this thing stuffed in your ear?" He said, as he pulled a silver coin from her ear. "Oh, I see, it is a magic nickel!"

He grinned again, as he pushed the nickel into her hand, and when she raised her head in surprise, I got a good chance to look into her eyes, and felt an almost electric jolt from what I read there.

When, we got into the car, the sheriff turned on the motor, but then turned to me. "Well, what did you think?"

I had to organize my thoughts, so to buy time for that, blurted out "I saw how you pulled that nickel from your palm."

The sheriff sighed, "Yeah, an old car-nie's trick. Good way to get kids to lighten up, but what about Suzie?"

"Well, she does love her father, but he makes her do things for him that are bad. He used to do that with Judy, but then, she got to be a teenager, and wasn't home much, so he started on the younger daughter. She doesn't like it, but she loves him, and he is sick and hurting, and kept telling her it would make him feel better."

Now I had the sheriff's complete attention, as he asked quietly, "What kind of things?"

In spite of myself, I could feel a hot uncomfortable fire rise to my cheeks. Somehow, looking at the dead woman hadn't been too hard, but this was a totally taboo area.

"You know, like sex things." I knew now that my blush was a fierce red, and in a

way that childish blush embarrassed me almost as much as having to tell him all this.

 # Chapter 36

THE LADIES
PREPARE FOR GUESTS

Dinner at my grandma's house that night was a welcome relief from all the tension of trying to read what the people around me were doing, and having to explain that stuff to the sheriff without sounding like a complete "witchy woman" myself.

Angelique had packed earlier in the day to catch the evening Greyhound out to go north to her next assignment. Then, she and Grandma had worked together, making a chicken and dumplings dinner, and exchanging comfortable gossip about their individual cooking styles. After they had finished eating, they settled, smiling, to watch me enjoy my second helping of their art.

We were all still lingering at the table, when Angelique's head suddenly shot up, and her eyes widened.

When I listened, I heard what she had heard. A very slow, very deliberate rattle on the gravel was coming down the little dead end lane where Grandma's house set. Looking out the side curtain, I could see a battered, dusty pick-up truck drive by slowly with men peering suspiciously from the windows.

"Keep away from the windows." Angelique's voice was a tight urgent hiss, as she pulled me down below the window pane.

The truck passed to the end of the lane, then made a u-turn and came back by slowly, with the men crowded in the cab really looking at our house now. It almost stopped, then speeded up and left, down toward the main part of town, spraying gravel.

"They'll be back tonight. They won't do anything in daylight, but it is going to be dark soon, and when..." Angelique was in a panic now, going from room to room, closing all the curtains and unscrewing all the light bulbs except for porch light.

"Maybe we should leave, so we won't get Grandma in trouble."

"Too late, they will be somewhere where they can watch the street. And if they got us, they would have to come back and make sure she wasn't able to tell anything."

"Keep the lights off! Miss Tennie, do you have a gun?"

"No, not really. Have my father's long-tom, but don't think we have any shells for it. You know, they probably stopped making them years ago. Never thought we would need a gun now, living in town and all."

Angelique took a deep sigh, then, muttered, almost to herself "Damn! The one time I had to be on the road without backup, but who would have thought you would need it in this little backwater burg?! Mary, get your grandma and get back in the bedroom. Lock the door and don't come out unless I tell you."

Humming softly to herself, Angelique slid grandma's chicken-cleaning knife in the back waistband of her skirt, and two smaller knives in the full pockets of the front of her skirt. The big butcher knife, she laid on the coffee table, under a loose newspaper while the really sharp little blade that grandma used to prune plants she held hidden in her left hand.

There was loud rattling coming back down the overgrown lane. Then a cloud of flying dead leaves and dust spun by the porch screen door while headlights flashed through the front windows and circled the walls. In a moment, there was the sound of heavy boots on the loose boards of the porch. I grabbed my grandma and hugged her face to my shoulder, while Angelique flattened herself against the wall by the door, as the knob started to rattle angrily.

Chapter 37

A Short Ride through a Dark Town

"Mary! I know you girls are in there. Now get out here this minute." My father's voice seemed to reverberate in the small house, and seemed at odds with his bellowed instructions to be quiet when he yelled next, "Keep the lights off and keep quiet and com'on!"

"Dad, what are you doing here?"

"I got a call from the sheriff that you girls had gone and gotten yourself into some sort of serious, stupid trouble. He is still at the court house, and needed me to cover for him until we can get your friend out of town."

"Tennie, you stay here, and don't

turn the lights on after we leave. If they see us going through town, they won't be coming back here to bother you. But, stay away from the windows!"

As we slid into the truck, I noticed in the dim of the moonlight a dark figure crouched in the back of the dusty pickup. When I leaned over to peer closely, Mr. Leroy's voice whispered out of the dark. "Don't worry, Mary, it is only me. I came along with your dad in case he needed backup getting your friend out of town." In the filtered moonlight, I could make out a glint off the long shape of the rifle he carried.

Dad turned the engine over and started to roll slowly down the dark lane in the moonlight without turning the headlights on. "Now, girls, if we meet anybody going across town, Angelique you duck down. Mary, if there is shooting, I want you to get down as low as you can as well. I figure after we get out to the highway, they won't be trying to stop us. There are lights there, and folks driving by."

A single light on the main corner of the town center was on. It seemed to flicker, but still gave enough light by working with the moonlight to show that the streets were strangely empty and deserted. The street lights that normally lit the side streets until nine each evening were blank and dark. Porches that should have held folks sitting in the evening air and gossiping with their neighbors, were now gapingly empty, with the front doors closed, and curtains drawn, but I still felt the silent eyes of the townspeople that I knew were peering out from behind those drawn lacy curtains.

Several blocks past the dark houses, the revival church spilled light out onto its steps and the crowd of scowling members, that watched our truck roll silently by. There was a small gathering of men milling around the steps of the church, and I recognized a few that I knew would try to hurt Angelique if they had known she was crouched between our feet in the old truck. The men glared over at the truck and waves of suspicion and hate seemed to erase the gleaming of the after-church-on-a-Sunday evening glow.

"Hey, you!"

My dad rolled the truck to a stop. "Well, Ed Mentz..., what the hell do you want?"

Mr. Mentz stepped back from the truck a bit. "Sorry, Mr. Randolph, didn't know it was you. You seen a nigger man dressed up funny running around town tonight?" From her lair between our feet, I heard Angelique hiss and could feel her body tense.

"Mentz, do I look like I'm out looking for stray niggers for you guys to rough up?! My daughter and I are just going over to meet the bus, and pick up some cholera shot medicine for my pigs." He growled, "And I will thank you men to get out of my way, or I'm going to roll this old truck right over you. She is pretty banged up, already, so a few more peckerhead dents in the paint aren't going to hurt one way or the other."

"Okay, okay, Mr. Randolph. No need to get mad. Hey! Did you know your head-lights aren't on?"

My dad's answer to that was to rev the engine and start to roll forward through the crowd that separated around the front of the truck.

Dad rolled on down the long darkened street a couple of blocks to the one light at the end of the street, the bus station. Near the end of the block, the huge Catholic church on the edge of town loomed tall and seemingly sanctified. His-torically, I knew from my reading it was supposed to be a refuge for those in trouble, but the doors were massive and locked in the dark. Even here on the outer edge of town, the street lights were still off, for some reason, but my dad could peer ahead at the station out on the highway, glowing with bright promising lights.

As Dad slowed, Mr. Leroy slid out of the back of the truck and whispered to my dad. "I'm going to be over there behind those bushes where I can keep a good view of the street and the station. Now, don't you forget to pick me up when she leaves. I wouldn't want to be caught on foot in this town with a rifle tonight, and I sure couldn't expect to slip out of town unnoticed in day-light!"

Dad growled again and waved him away without looking away from peering through the dirty windshield at the seem-ingly deserted bus station.

"Dammit Leroy! You know I'll be back

to pick you up! Just keep out of sight and rub some dust on that gun barrel so it doesn't shine if the moon comes back out."

"You trying to tell me how to keep out of sight? Maybe you'd like me to rub a little dust all over me, too?!"

In the dark cab of the truck, Angelique's hand squeezed mine. She whispered, "Mr. Randolph, I am real sorry to have caused you folks all this trouble. I thought I'd just stop in and visit with Mary, then leave. Forgot how things could get in little towns like this."

My father didn't glance around as he rolled the old truck through the silent dark streets to the lighted platform of the station. He had kept the headlights off, and was peering carefully ahead in a fitful moonlight. "Look, Miss Angelique. I know our town is not what it should be and folks in the south are not always what they should be. Maybe in Mary's lifetime that will all change, but right now, ol' Jim Crow is still alive and well here. Whether that is right or wrong isn't something I can argue about, now. Not my job right now. Getting you out of here alive and Mary home safe is."

Dad's jaw snapped closed in the grim line that I knew so well. For him, at least, that was the last word in the conversation..., in any conversation.

Chapter 38

A FAREWELL TO FRIENDS... AGAIN

The bus pulled into the lighted patch of the station. There didn't seem to be many folks on board. Then, the doors swung open and the muscular brown uniformed driver swooped down and grabbed Angelique's bag and swung it into the luggage bay under the bus, all in one smooth motion. Then he turned to Angelique.

"Angelique! Honey, what in the hell were you thinking of to get stuck here in this mess?!" as he grabbed her and hugged her tight.

My father's jaw dropped in amazement at this greeting. Then, the driver turned around to face us and I found myself looking up into the familiar, Korean grin of my friend, Jimmy Pak.

"Hi, Miss Mary Randolph! Good to see you again!" Another hug. Over his broad shoulder, I could see my father's face, still a classic study in the drama of amazement.

Then Jimmy turned to my dad and grabbed his hand in both hands and shook it fiercely. "Sir, the US government is so grateful to you for taking care of our agent and not letting this situation get out of hand! The President said to give you his gratitude and personal thanks, and that goes double for me! Miss Angelique is one of our top American agents. And she is just the finest woman to ever come into my life!"

With that, he seized my dad, laid a massive hard sweaty Korean hug on him, and grabbing Angelique by the arm, swung her up onto the steps of the still running bus.

As I said good bye to Angelique and Jimmy, and the bus started to roll away, it paused and the doors swung open again, and Angelique called me over. She stood on the step hanging on to the rail, as Jimmy peered out through the windshield at the dark road ahead. Unmindful of his urgings to get back in the bus, she reached behind her to pull out grandma's chicken cleaning butcher knife and handed it to me.

"Here, give this back to your grandma; she'll be needing it. Tell her I love her, and I kept one of her little paring knives, but I'll get it back to her, someday. Just need something to carry on the road with me. A girl can't be too careful!"

Then she laughed. "Oh, honey, do you realize this is the first time I have spent any length of time with you and not had to kill someone?!"

She hugged me again, and I felt that strangely rough cheek on mine. "You are such a special person, Mary. Just always stay as sweet as you are."

"Sweet?" I was not sure how that applied to me, when my dad, and the invisible Mr. Leroy, had been the ones to keep the bad things from happening, but I waved at them, and kept the goodbye tears from welling until they were on the road and roaring off into the dark night and their future.

"Mary, who are these people!? And how do they know you so well? And what the hell is a Jap doing in our government secret service anyway?!"

"He is an American agent of Korean descent, Dad. And he is from Ohio." I hoped that would be enough to distract Dad from further questions until I could think up answers for him, but had a feeling that wasn't going to be the case.

He was still mulling it over when we stopped by the bushes behind the church, and a dark shadow slid from the darker shadows of the crepe myrtles and into the dimness in the back of the truck.

A moment later, Mr. Leroy's face loomed, peering in the window behind the truck cab.

"Randolph, what happened back there? I couldn't see it very well, but looked like a Jap or somebody grabbed our girl."

"He wasn't a Jap; he was an American Korean and a very important member of our secret service of the United States of America!" My dad sounded a little smug in his knowledge.

The town was still dark when we drove back across it. The street lights were still mysteriously blank, but by the light of the moon slipping in and out of the clouds it was obvious that the self-proclaimed warrior militia were out elsewhere hunting dark skinned prey. The lights from the tavern window on Main Street were a hint at where that would be.

"So, Dad, how did you know we needed help?"

"Your boss, the sheriff, heard what was going to happen if you stayed at Tennie's house with your friend. He is over at the court house, having an after-work meeting with the judge and couldn't get out of there and across the hills in time to help you. He knew I didn't have a phone, so he called Leroy, who came and got me. Silly nigger, I think he would have gone to save you all by himself, except he knew he wouldn't be able to stop them alone. I told him those boys would really enjoy watching two black hanging corpses swinging in the light when Tennie's house went up in flames if he wanted to be that stupid. So, anyway, we did what we had to do."

After we crossed the railroad tracks and turned down the little lane to my Grandma's house, we could see a bright exclamation point of light at the end of the dark street. When we got closer, we found Tennie, sitting on her front porch with the overhead bulb blazing down like a stage light in the dark. The huge old shot gun was lying quietly across her knees as she rocked in the old rocking chair that my grandpa's folks had brought across the mountains over a hundred years ago.

When we scolded her and made her turn off the light she said. "I'm not going to be bothered by those peckerheads! They are evil, cowardly toads. But, I do want them to know if they come here, they are going to get hurt."

 # Chapter 39

DIRTY LAUNDRY

After successfully getting Angelique out of town in one piece, and without having to kill someone, I was hoping not to see the sheriff for a few days. I was a little burned out with all the guilt and worrying about Mrs. Talbot and this tangled case in general. I thought my suggestion of letting her be released to the care of her granddaughters and not putting anyone into prison for this death would direct things the way they should go.

That death almost seemed less than a murder to me now. Hadn't the girls' mother been planning to take the family money, and wouldn't that leave them having to plan on working for a living like the rest of us? Somehow, the logic they would use on this situation made it seem almost plausible and necessary to murder their mother.

Now, I couldn't put the darkness of Suzie's relationship with her father out of my mind. Somehow, without her telling me, I knew that she did things for him that he told her would make him feel better. Not old enough to speak up, and too afraid of him, she was dirtied, ashamed and alone in this situation. Her mother, who should have been the one to see, and stop this, had deserted her for the freedom and fun of having time away from a mean domineering man to spend with her student. Judy, who knew what he was capable of, was also enjoying new horizons of teenaged glamour and boys, without the restraints of dealing with that sick, evil father, so she chose to ignore her sister's lonely time in the trenches.

So, as tired as I was getting of hanging out with the sheriff and seeing all these sad lives work out, the next morning, instead of going all the way to the high school, I asked Mr. Emerson to drop me near the city hall where the sheriff had his office. Mr. Emerson, our one eyed bus driver, had by now gotten pretty used to my strange requests, and over the years, had gotten used to, I guess, being more or less my private chauffeur. He only tilted one eyebrow over his good eye, or at least the one I always thought was his good eye, and nodded silently.

"We really need to go back to Judy's house!" Nothing to be gained by beating around the bush, as I pushed the wood and glass door to the sheriff's office open, and charged in.

Loudly, "No time to beat around the bush," I proclaimed, "Com'on, we have to get over to Judy's house, now!"

His chair legs hit the floor with a bang, as he sat up, splashing the cup of coffee in his hand on his morning paper.

"And should I ask what the hell for, young lady?"

"No, that would just take time, and I think we need to get over there as soon as we can."

Pulling on his jacket, and wiping at the coffee splatters on his pants, he rushed to open the door for me and herd me down to the county car.

"Yeah, I was thinking about what you said about that sex stuff and about to decide the same thing. Usually, we just let the families handle that sort of thing without the law messing in it, but this seems sort of like a case where we should step in. She is just a little girl, after all."

"And, she isn't his first."

 # Chapter 40

THE MUSIC PLAYED ON

When we pulled up in front of Judy's house I was surprised to see the druggist, Mr. Huffman, and Judy huddled together on her porch talking animatedly in the sunshine. From the open window, the liquid notes of some classic piece that I had heard Judy's mother play in a past recital, seemed to float out on the warm air in an insistent twirl of notes.

Mr. Huffman came down the steps to meet us, his face tight and pale. "I was just going to call you."

For once, his seemingly calm manner was gone, and his voice was quavering. "Judy called me when she found her father. Her mother is dazed, and she didn't know what to do."

"Found her father!? What's going on here?" The sheriff cleared the front steps and the porch seemingly in one rush, but I was ahead of him, holding the door open and peering into the darkened interior, as the lovely classical music rippled on and on.

"He's upstairs." Judy's face was pale and stiff, her lips seeming to move on their own. She led us up the carpeted steps to the room across from the stairs. There seemed to be three other rooms on that floor, with an open door to the bathroom lit by an old stained glass window.

We entered the dim room with the sheriff leading the way, and me close behind him. Mr. Huffman had stopped at the bottom of the stairs next to the open door of the studio where Judy's mother continued to pour out the long, continuous music, protecting herself, I supposed, from the world outside her piano. Judy stood, silently at the open door.

The smell in the room was an appalling acid smell, that I realized, when I saw the body, was from the puddle of urine on the soaked bed sheets it was lying in. The limbs, as the poisoned animals I had seen with the vet, were twisted and the whole torso seemed tortured and frozen in a final spasm of pain.

The face was also frozen in an expression of agony and seemed to have been caught in a final expression of pain and silent pleading. Somehow, I felt that the man, evil as he was, had known he was dying and why. He seemed to have died pleading with a world that was finished putting up with his sins, for just one more chance.

The sheriff turned to Judy at the door of the room. "Where is your sister?"

"I guess she slept in. I haven't seen her this morning." Judy's face was still stiff and pale, and I knew that there was more here then she wanted to deal with.

"Where's her room? We need to talk to her as well as you. Then we will have to get the coroner over here."

Judy nodded at a door down the hall, without speaking, and I went down to it, and knocked lightly on it. "Suzie, honey, this is Mary Randolph. The sheriff is here, too, and we have to talk to you again. It's real important."

The only sound was the notes from the music downstairs, and the dark silence behind the door that seemed to speak out louder than any noise would have.

"I'll go in." The sheriff was beside me, now, and I could read the apprehension in his face and body, as he quietly opened the door and we went into the room.

Suzie was sitting on the floor by her bed, leaned back against a pile of stuffed toys and pillows. Her face was cold and waxy, and a striking contrast to the unbelievably large congealed puddle of blood about her on the floor. Looking at her, the first thought that came into my shocked mind was to wonder how a human body could contain so much blood. Especially such a little girl form of a human body.

The sheriff's hand on my arm was a steel claw. "Oh good God!" As he drug me from the room, and softly closed the door.

"That poor little girl, that poor, poor little girl!" The sheriff mustered up and used all his wits in getting me away from those doors and down the stairs. On the porch, he pressed me down onto a chair, though I suspected his own shock was as deep as mine.

And in the parlor, Judy's mother's music played on.

Chapter 41

HARLAND REMEMBERS A TROPICAL ISLE

Harland Philips carefully hung up his robe. *Another day of impossible decisions, and tangled problems. The deserved, but questionable death of a man who had been doing foul things to his daughters, and his poor pregnant little daughter that died from a gone-wrong corrective abortion and probably from shame. What a headache!*

Now, after that was all more or less sorted out, his friend, Sheriff Olsen had deserted him so that he couldn't even have an after work unwinding drink without feeling like a lush for drinking alone.

O well, lush be damned. Sometimes a man just needs a drink, he thought as he pulled out the least dusty of the two glasses he kept in the bottom drawer next to the bottle and his gun when he wasn't wearing it under the judicial robes.

Damned! Day like today and I'll probably be dreaming about those damned bananas again!

Those bananas; funny when I was a kid bananas were a real treat. Remember Aunt Mary Lou's banana pudding. Made with store bought vanilla cookies and pudding with bananas sliced all through it, and layered together, then baked in the oven until the fluffy meringue on top was brown and shiny with drops of syrup glistening on it.

Man, when I was twelve that was real good eating!

But when I was twenty, and a scared young Marine hiding in the jungle behind the Jap lines on that Pacific island and creeping out at night to look for food, that all changed. I had been scratched and scraped from hiding in the jungle, and had two slight bullet grazes from the battle. One was on the side of my neck and then there was the one across my scalp that had probably saved my life. After the battle, I had lain stunned and bloody surrounded by the dead bodies of the other Marines in my platoon. Somehow, when the Jap soldiers came up to us, I could hear them laughing and finishing off some of the boys who weren't dead, but they must have not noticed me. After they left, I crawled over into the low underbrush and hid without moving until dark, when I found what I thought was a safer spot. My wounds were sore and infected by now, and I could feel maggots in the scalp wound, so knew it was just a matter of time until the wounds got me, even without the Japs.

The food foraging part didn't come until after I had been wallowing in the muddy swamp for several days. Too scared *at first to even think about food, I had managed to find some water that I thought wouldn't kill me under the brush at the edge of the mud. But finally I got desperate enough to take a chance on being spotted by the Japanese patrols.*

Got a couple of green bananas the first night; made me sick at my stomach. But the second night I went back, planning to hunt for some riper ones that I could hold in my stomach long enough to take some strength from them before they gave me massive diarrhea.

My banana stealing skills weren't that good, and I probably would have died in a few painful days, if I hadn't been caught by that little brown farmer whose bananas I was trying to tear off before his dog raised too much alarm. He saw me, and switched from yelling in outrage to concern for me. He hid me in a bamboo lean-to behind his tool shed, and washed up the wounds, pick-

ing out the maggots. Then, bless him, he fed me some rice gruel. I knew I was taking food that his family needed, but was so grateful. And he never spoke of his danger from helping me, but a few days later; he grabbed me roughly without speaking, pulled me out, shoved me back under the thick roots of the banana stalks, and pushed leaves and dirt over me. A few minutes later, I heard the screaming as the Japs came into his compound. They were yelling at him in front of his family. Then, they made him kneel down. A few minutes later, when his head rolled on the ground, his eyes seemed to be looking toward me in my hiding place in the banana grove, and there seemed to be a slight, triumphant smile around his lifeless lips.

'Course, the Japs never found me, but a lot of people suffered for protecting me.

And I could never even smell bananas without the return of the breathless terror of that day. Months of therapy after the war, and even went on to law school, before sinking into the safety net of being the judge in this quiet little rural county. But too much stress or the smell of bananas and I still am that scared wounded kid that watched in silent horror as his benefactor was being killed.

Hands slightly trembling at the re-played memories, Harland reached for his friend in the bottle, just as the door slammed open, and the red-headed vet roared into the room.

"Harland, you dummy! If that Mary Randolph hadn't been asking me questions about arsenic poisoning, I might have missed the whole thing!"

"Madam, I will thank you to get out of my office. It is after hours and I am just getting ready to leave for the day."

The smell of hay and horses seemed to mingle with indignation as she ignored

Harland, and continued. "Judge! What's the matter with you? Don't you know I am just a vet, not a human doctor? I don't get paid for this job, and sometimes I make mistakes. Why can't you get a regular doctor and pay him a little to do this, instead of having me bumbling along. Shouldn't cost you too much..., not a real hard job. After all, his patients wouldn't be talking back, and he probably wouldn't be risking a cat scratch or dog bite on the job."

Now her steam of ire seemed to have run out now, as she stared at the shocked, invaded man behind the desk.

Then, shoulders drooping, glancing off at the framed certificates on the wall behind Harland, "Judge, you married?"

"Uhh, no."

"Good! The truth is, then, that you are not really in that great of a hurry to go home. So, I will join you for a little sip of whatever that was that you pushed into your file drawer when I walked in. Think it is time we get to know each other, if I am going to have to be working with you."

"Madam!" Judges aren't supposed to ever sputter or be at a loss for words, but Harland felt himself almost sputtering in indignation and really, somewhat at a loss for words.

"And I need to talk to you about this dead lady you sent to my morgue. She didn't die of a gunshot, you know."

"Not shot! But I saw that body myself. And I have seen enough dead bodies in the war to know what a gunshot looks like!"

The vet lowered her butt onto the comfortable chair, and slipping off sensible, low heeled shoes, and tucking her skirt demurely around her knees, propped her feet up on Harland's desk and smiled sweetly at him.

"Okay, your Honor, I will take that drink now."

Chapter 42

MOTHER LOVES BLUE FLOWERS

They had the funeral for Judy's father the next Saturday, followed by a small service for Suzie the next day.

Judy's father's turnout was pretty good. He had, at one time, been a respected businessman around the community and had attended church regularly and conspicuously, until his illness. No one seemed real sure of what his illness had been, but there was a general agreement that he had been a valued member of the community. Kept his yard real neat, too; before his illness.

His wife was too distraught to attend his services, but Judy was there representing the family. I barely got to speak to her because of the numerous other folks who were filing past the painted husk in the coffin, but she seemed to be totally handling things well, smiling and murmuring to the mourners. There were clouds of blue hydrangeas around the room and the coffin, wafting a soft cloying scent through the room. Judy's Marine boyfriend was there, too, but I didn't really get to meet him until the next day, when they had the service for Suzie.

Suzie's service was in the same funeral home, but was limited to immediate family and a few invited guests. For some reason, I was included in the invited guests. They had kept the same blue flowers from the first funeral, and this time, Judy's mother had showed up, and sat silently in the front row, crying softly into a hankie. The druggist, Mr. Huffman, sat equally silent, beside her. She didn't speak to any of the rest of us, and never seemed to look toward the closed coffin. The thought had occurred to me that if the girls were in a 'coven' with a leader; possibly their mother, or even Mr. Huffman, might be guiding them, but now, they were just two tired, middle-aged people who were sitting sad faced and empty at a funeral.

The sheriff had told me that Suzie had died from trying to abort the early pregnancy she had been carrying. I wondered if she had found out about the powers of the pennyroyal, or the other plants, and which one of the girls trying to be witches had told her about that. Or, if there was a wire clothes hanger involved as I had heard whispered about at times in the girls bathroom at school. One of those advantages of a high school education, I supposed.

It seemed that Mrs. Talbot had also made the cut for those invited to this funeral. She sat, in her Sunday clothes, even with a flowered hat, between her two grand-daughters. Brenda and Betty were silently each holding one of her gloved hands, and even patted her occasionally. For such a pitifully sad time, she looked remarkably happy.

The other interesting hold over from the first funeral, beside the blue flowers, was the presence of the neatly uniformed Marine that stood by Judy's side through the brief ceremony. Somehow, in the face of all this bizarre small town doings and these strange deaths, he had upheld the traditions of the Marine Corps honorably, standing straight with chin tucked and answering in brief matter-of-fact terseness when spoken to, sprinkling all his statements with lots of "Sirs" and "Ma'ams" the way most of the folks thought a well raised young man should.

Judy led me over to meet him, and hissed under her social smile to me, "He is a real lance corporal. That means he is a real official non commissioned officer! But in a few months, he may get to go to Officer School to become a gentleman, and they may make him a helicopter pilot, even. If that happens, he might be going over to Asia where they are having all that trouble. At least he won't be on the ground fighting there. He'll just fly over the ground fighting and pick up the wounded heroes. They won't even shoot at him! And, Mary, if I become an officer's wife, they have all those fancy tea parties and real balls, where they wear real long formal gowns, not like these silly proms we get to have in the high school gym every year."

The man under the uniform was a surprise in more ways than one, though. He was obviously young, probably only a couple of years older than Judy and me. Fairly tall, his scrawny wrists seemed to noticeably protrude out of his shirt cuffs, supporting his bony long fingered hands. Despite his proud military bearing, he still bore traces of leftover teenage acne that seemed to be covered by some flesh colored cream. Though mostly looking straight ahead, when I spoke to him, he responded by turning large, almost frightened eyes peering at me through thick glass lenses.

Those wide eyes seemed to speak to me, and when I took his hand, I had a quick vision of him dying, bloody and hurt on the edge of a rice paddy in a far off land, with strange non-American uniformed warriors surrounding him. His last view of the world, was of his thick glasses, reflecting his numb face in a broken lens.

Trying to bring my thoughts back from that dark image, I whispered to Judy as we went out into the sunshine. "All those vases of hydrangeas. They're pretty showy for a casket, aren't they?"

Her face, when she turned to answer

me in the bright light in front of the chapel was the same as always, calm and serene, with carefully applied make-up and perfect, unruffled hair. Her smile was smooth, bland and beautiful, as befitted a maybe future wife of an officer and official gentleman. But behind the softness of her blue eyes, I could see the bottomless, pitiless darkness that I had only seen before in the evil eyes of my father's killer boar.

"Why, Mary, I've told you before. Mother just loves those blue flowers."

Chapter 43

HARLAND STAYS ALERT

A few days after those horrible funerals, Harland again settled his tired feet on his desk and cradled a small end-of-the-day shot of his favorite unwinding beverage. *Not a bad day. Got to the bottom of all those bodies popping up all over the place, and even figured out how to handle everything in a humane, just way. Sure, he had to sentence the old lady for supposedly shooting her daughter... Granny had insisted on taking the blame for that. "You decide, Harland. I'm 87 years old, and I am going to die no matter what you do to me. And if you put my granddaughters in jail it will just kill me faster, and turn them into terrible people." So, on the sage advice of his friend, the sheriff, he finally pronounced her guilty and had her declared mentally incompetent, then slapped her elderly butt into the local nut house on an out patient basis and released her on probation to her home under the total care and supervision of the granddaughters that she had tried so hard to protect.*

So, for the most part, Harland was pretty satisfied with how he had handled a knotty problem. Somehow the sheriff had figured out that it was the murdered woman's daughters who had poisoned their mother, and Granny had shot her body, *her own daughter!* to try to hide the fact that she had been poisoned, and lead the death away from her granddaughters. After all, Harland thought, what law had she broken? Maybe only tampering with evidence, maybe only lying to the court, and what is this hogwash of shooting a dead body of a relative!? But, the bottom line was that she is a very old lady, and her main crime was loving her undeserving granddaughters too much, and trying to protect them.

That train of thought brought him back to a point he had nagging in the back of his mind. Did Dr. Grace really miss that poisoning, or had she tried to cover up the cause of death to spare the family? He knew she didn't want to work with dead bodies, but he sort of wanted her to continue as coroner for awhile.

Hmm, sidebar..., Dr. Grace.

Sipping the last of his whiskey, he paused and reconsidered his findings. *Damned, that Mary Randolph is one smart little gal... seemed to know how this was all going to work out. Sure glad the sheriff has her to fall back on.*

Hmm, Dr. Grace seems to always have that silly run sneaking up her no nonsense hose, and a tendril of red hair blowing in her face as she works.

Maybe it is time I go across the street and talk to her about that run. An official of the court has to always be alert.

The end...

Coming Soon

A Mary Randolph adventure

TO KEEP

A DARK PROMISE

 **Prologue**

MOONWALKER GETS A CALL

"Perry, she's back."

The old wood farm house was cold with a pre dawn chill, and out the windows, he could see the garlic fields stretching in the leftover moonlight.

"What do you mean she's back, and

do you know what time it is?!"

"Perry, she walked into my dream, and sat down in the corner of the dark room and just sat there with her head drooping. Only she wasn't the Marilyn we knew as a grown up. She was a little girl, and she was dust streaked and dirty. Her clothes were shabby and torn and she just sat there in the corner on a stool with her head hanging down, crying. Finally I got up the nerve to approach her, and she looked up at me. Her face wasn't frightening, though. It was just the face of a tired, hurt child, and I wiped the dust and tears off her cheeks."

"Please, please," she whispered, so quietly I could barely hear her. "Call Mary."

"Mary?" I said. "Who's Mary?"

"Mary Randolph", she whispered still so faintly I could barely hear her. "I need to talk to Mary Randolph."

Margaret P Nelson

Mary Randolph Adventures

THE GIRL FROM THE DITCH DUMP ROAD

TRILOGY:

1949 – QUILT PIECES

1953 – RUBY AND THE YELLOW ROSE

1957 – MARY'S ROAD

And

1958 – MOTHER LOVES BLUE FLOWERS

1963 – TO KEEP A DARK PROMISE
(AVAILABLE – FALL 2014)

Other Stories

THE LABS THAT SAVED CHRISTMAS (AVAILABLE – FALL 2014)

TALES OF THE IRON HORSE MANOR
(AVAILABLE – FALL 2014)

Margaret P Nelson was born in Lutesville, Missouri and grew up on a small farm in Southeast Missouri. She graduated from The University of Guam in 1980. She traveled extensively in Southeast Asia for her businesses. She also lived in Korea, Spain, Bermuda, and Guantanamo Bay, Cuba. She had two sons and currently lives in the Ozarks with her editor and three black labs. She is writing the next Mary Randolph adventure and other stories.

Margaret's books are also available as ebooks from Amazon-Kindle.

Made in the USA
San Bernardino, CA
08 February 2014